RIZE SHORT STORY ANTHOLOGY
VOLUME 1

RUNNING
Wild
PRESS

RIZE

Short Story Anthology

Volume 1
text copyright © remains with authors
Edited by Benjamin B. White

Published in North America and Europe by RIZE Press. Visit Running Wild Press at www.runningwildpress.com, Educators, librarians, book clubs (as well as the eternally curious), go to www.runningwildpress.com.

ISBN (pbk) 978-1-960018-11-3

ISBN (ebook) 978-1-960018-10-6

CONTENTS

THERE WILL COME A TRAIN

BY FENG GOOI

The sun lashed against my back like a cruel whip, my muscles wailed in agony, begging for just one moment of respite yet I could not stop. I had no choice, stopping meant death. My calloused hands gripped my shovel, smashed it against the stubborn Siamese dirt and dug again and again to cut a path out of this impossible terrain. I had been here long enough to have seen what happened when someone stopped and broke down, a single second of rest would turn into a long march of slow withering death. Whether by disease or fatigue, once you had succumbed to the yearning, you would fall and never get up again.

So, despite the pain, despite the exhaustion, despite the torture of my soul, I worked. The four of us, Yan Long, Zi Han, Soon Ong and me, knew this and that's why we survived thus far while the rest of our original party of Chinese Malayan workers died off one by one.

At least, that's what I told myself.

I looked to my right to make sure Soon Ong was still working. He appeared to be, he swung his shovel into the earth with

1

furious strength, but the oozing rot of flesh below his right knee made me wince. He had gotten a cut in an accident a few days earlier and it was infected with a jungle ulcer. I was no doctor, but Soon Ong was a big bull of a man, if anyone could tough out and survive an infection he could.

For a moment, I hoped.

We were the *romusha,* the 'voluntary' civilian workforce, for this grand engineering project under the Empire of Japan, a four-hundred-kilometer railway between Siam and Burma cutting through impenetrable tropical rainforest, wild raging rivers and harsh steep mountains. At first the Japanese were able to lure workers on the false promise of good work and pay, but soon enough, as thousands upon thousands died under the harsh brutal conditions, the Japanese coerced and kidnapped young healthy men from across Asia to slave away on this railroad of death.

A slow procession of white prisoners of war were marched past us to complete some other task for the railroad. At the tail end, Yan Long spit on the ground and muttered, "British dogs," in English.

One of the prisoners heard him and turned back. I feared a tussle, but the white prisoner, his uniform now nothing but tatters, his body a skeleton with a bloated stomach, just looked at him with sad tired eyes and said, "I'm Australian."

It was amazing to consider all the different nationalities and ethnicities across the world gathered here in these jungles where no man belonged. Dutch, British, Australian, American, Siamese, Burmese, Javanese, Indian, Sumatran, Chinese, Malay, Japanese, and Korean. There were thousands of us in this very section of the line, thousands of shovels, hoes, pickaxes and hammers smashing against rock and dirt. We were initially segregated by race, but as our party died out we were integrated with a group of Tamil Indian and Muslim Malay newcomers.

Despite sharing the homeland of Malaya and slaving away on the same bone breaking task, the four of us Chinese Malayans kept to ourselves. It was partly due to racial animosity but also due to a simple fact, the less you know about someone, the easier it was to bury them.

"Why the hell did you say that?" I asked Yan Long quietly.

"Those Western capitalist dogs, they come here, rape the land, they feast on its bounty while the people starve and then they tuck their tails, and let these Japanese bastards' rape and massacre our people in turn. They deserve much more than harsh words, Foo Xian," Yan Long said.

His voice was quiet yet simmering with unbridled rage. Yan Long had a tall and lean build. He was a former Communist guerrilla fighting against the Imperial army in the jungles of Malaya until he was caught and shipped here.

"Does it really matter? They're suffering, we're suffering. We're all suffering together here."

"Yet even here our suffering is unequal."

This was partially true. Though I've witnessed the cruelties and torture Japanese soldiers inflicted upon the prisoners, the Japanese still attempted some weak feeble adherence to the conventions of war. On the other hand, our accommodations, tasks, and rations were even worse than the prisoners. The Japanese officers saw us as less than human. We were mules, machines to be used till we were broken and then tossed aside. Ironic, given the Japanese marched into Malaya promising to free us from the colonizers under the banner of "Asia for Asians".

"No use thinking about all the inequalities of the world. You'll go crazy Yan Long," Soon Ong said.

"I'm a communist, that's all I think about when I'm not imagining tearing these Japanese pigs' limb to limb," he said with a quick glare at the bored Japanese officers supervising us.

"Well, better keep dreaming Yan Long. You're not killing anyone soon," Soon Ong said.

"That's not true. Three days from today, Yan Long will kill you. He'll split your head open and all the bright red blood will seep into soil. It'll feed the trees," said Zi Han suddenly in a strange, disquieting voice.

Zi Han was the youngest of the group, only sixteen years old. He had only been there in the Southern reaches of the world for three years. His family had fled China to escape the Japanese occupation, only to end up there, halfway across the globe and still crushed under their inescapable boots. What a sad joke. He was a quiet and shy boy, and the three of us were very protective of him.

"W-What did you just say Zi Han?" I asked. The rest of us looked at each other briefly in confusion and alarm.

I looked at the boy, he continued plunging his shovel into the dirt, but his eyes were glazed and distant, his entire face cold and expressionless. Then, just like that, he snapped back.

"What?" he asked casually.

"What you said, what were you..."

My questioning was cut short by the shouts of a Japanese officer. I didn't understand a single word of the language but knew I had to shut my mouth now. So, I continued working, digging again and again until Zi Han's odd statement faded from my mind.

* * *

The night was cool and serene, the soft chittering of cicadas filled my ears like a soothing lullaby. Some nights made you shiver, some nights made you sweat and moan, some nights the mosquitoes swarmed and feasted on your blood. The worst nights were when it rained, the tiny tent the twenty of us

Malayans were crammed into was shoddily made, the canvas would leak and drench us in cold rain water.

But tonight, was a good night. Still, I could not sleep. My body and spirit were ready to collapse and crumble into the joy of nothingness, but my mind would not relent. I glanced briefly into the darkness and realized that I wasn't the only one.

I saw the blurry shape of Yan Long in the shadows sitting with a knife in his hands, lovingly stroking it. I didn't know where or how he got the knife, but this wasn't the first time I witnessed his nightly ritual. If I strained my ears hard enough, I could hear the almost unintelligible whispers of all the violence he wished to unleash upon his enemies.

Yan Long was a man who supped on the cup of hatred, it flowed down his throat and gave him the strength to endure. His entire village was massacred by the Japanese, bullets shredded their bodies to pieces, but he had escaped by sheer luck and began his path of righteous vengeance against them ever since. I had no doubt the hate was why he still lived when so many had died, rage powered his flesh and bones.

I knew why I still clung to life despite everything. I thought about them often, my wife and child. My son was only six months old when I was taken. I remembered how he giggled as he rolled around on his back, the cute sounds he made when I poked his soft baby cheeks. He must be walking now, saying his first words. I hoped despite my absence he found comfort in his mother's warm bosom. I missed her so much, her voice, her touch, her everything. Before the war, I had neglected her to focus on my business and soon I drowned in regret. The more I thought about them, the more worry plagued me.

Zi Han had told us about how he came to be there. How the Japanese soldiers came to his house to take his mother and sister to be comfort women, how he saw his father's stomach sliced open by their bayonets when he tried to stop them, how his sister and mother screamed when they saw his guts spill on the kitchen floor, how he just stood there frozen in fear. Zi Han told us this in a cold casualness that broke my heart.

I began praying that my wife and child were safe from such horrors, to Buddha, to whatever gods there were in the heavens. I was never a religious person before this. I fulfilled my obligations, burnt incense for the gods in the shrines, and offered abundant feasts for my ancestors, but I never truly believed. It's a sad cliche, I know, a man on the end of his rope searching for hope and comfort in religion, but I couldn't help thinking about karma, the pure concept of it.

Out there, burning and destroying my body under the sun, I looked back and examined my life, confronted every past transgression. Before all this, I was a businessman trading rice, powerful and successful for my young age, until the Japanese seized my business and sent me here. Foolishly, I assumed all my wealth would shield me from the harshest cruelties of the war. Now, all the precious material possessions I had accumulated were for naught. I thought about all the times I acted cruelly and callously in the name of profit, all the farmers I knowingly exploited, all the bad karma I had accumulated in my lifetime.

But were those sins worth the hell I suffered?

I wasn't a good man, but I wasn't an evil one either. Maybe I had been evil in a past life. Maybe my suffering was retribution for immoralities I no longer even remembered.

I thought about that a lot, past lives and future lives; our souls traversing from one body to the next, carrying the weight of sins of the past. It didn't really strike me as fair, but from my half haphazard understanding of Buddhism, it wasn't supposed to be, all life was suffering and pain, the goal was to break the cycle of agony and reincarnation, put an end to all the chaos of existence. But I wasn't concerned with that, all I prayed for was mercy for my wife and child. I prayed and prayed and prayed until eventually slumber took me in. For a moment, there was peace until the shrill blast of a whistle pulled me back into the cold light of day.

* * *

"Whoa! Careful there you almost took your toes off!" I said to Arif, a young Malay newcomer to the party. Despite the circumstances, he had an almost infectious aura of positivity. He always greeted everyone with a brilliant friendly smile.

"If you go on like that, you'll break your back in no time. Here, look at me, my posture. How I swing," I said. Our task of the day was breaking stones for ballast on the track and I demonstrated to Arif the way I smashed my hammer against the rocks. "Never thought a city boy like me would teach a kampung kid like you something like this."

"My father was the village chief, so I never had to do much hard work, honestly. But if you ever need someone to mediate between two bickering families, I'm your man," Arif laughed as he thanked me. Throughout all this I noticed Yan Long staring daggers at us.

"You shouldn't talk to those mongrels," he said to me in Chinese while Arif continued working, oblivious to his racist screed.

"Why the hell not?" I asked with a tired sigh.

"They're collaborators, good little helpers of the Japanese. Both them and the Indians," he said, giving the evil eye to the Indians in our party. "They stood aside while the Japanese monsters slaughtered our people, closed their eyes while we were rounded up. They happily worked with the Japanese while our businesses were ransacked and burnt to the ground. They're even serving in their police force. It's not the Malays or

Indians out there fighting against these Japanese bastards in Malaya. It's us!"

"Everyone's just trying to get by and there are Chinese collaborators, too, you know?"

"Yes, and they'll all get the bullet too. All those traitorous pigs gifting the Japanese $50 million," he said, referring to the 'atonement' the Japanese had made the Chinese businessmen pay for our 'sins' against the Empire.

"They had no choice! They were tortured! They were threatened with death, their families were threatened!"

"Excuses! There's always a choice! It won't save them when we reap our vengeance and slice the heads off those filthy capitalists."

A chill ran down my spine as I wondered if I was included in that category. "You're a collaborator too, you know?"

"What?!"

"You're here helping the Japanese build a railway so they can ship supplies to fight their war in Burma killing both the Burmese and our Chinese brothers."

Yan Long flushed red and stayed silent after that, but I could feel his rage radiating next to me. I feared it would be a long day of quiet resentment, but that was soon interrupted.

"Soon Ong! Are you doing alright?" Zi Han asked.

Soon Ong threw down his hammer and stood still for a moment, his face was ash white, his body was drenched in sweat. He collapsed onto the hard dirt floor and curled into a fetus position. I wasn't surprised, his condition had been getting worse for the past few days. It was inevitable, it was foolish of me to hope otherwise.

A Japanese officer saw this and began kicking the fallen Soon Ong, demanding he get up, but the man just continued lying in the dirt groaning. The soldier gave up and shouted at me and Yan Long to come over.

We both knew what we had to do and lifted Soon Ong off the ground, carrying him away from the indifferent crowd of workers. We began making our way to the 'coolie hospital' where there was much more dying than healing. There were hundreds of patients and only two British prisoner medics serving as doctors. Every morning twenty or more of the dead would be carted off from the shambling bamboo hut of a hospital into shallow graves where flies danced and feasted.

"No. Don't take me there, I don't want to die there," Soon Ong rasped through his dry cracked lips.

"Die? You're going to make it through, brother. The doctors will..."

"Don't bullshit me, Foo Xian! I'm dying and I know it. You know it. There's no hope for me. Just please don't take me there, don't let my last days be rotting away in that pit of death. End this for me."

Yan Long and I looked at each other and nodded. We crept away from the crowd and clatter to an isolated spot in the jungle where we laid Soon Ong down on a soft bed of grass. Yan Long picked up a large jagged rock.

"That'll do. Don't miss, make sure I die quickly," Soon Ong said.

"I've killed before," Yan Long replied.

"Is there anything you'd like us to tell your family?" I said crouching beside him.

Soon Ong gave a sad wistful smile, I could see he didn't believe we could ever do that. "I have no words. I'm too tired. I just want release."

He closed his eyes, and Yan Long smashed the rock down onto his head with surprising strength. It was like the stones we broke for ballast, but so much softer. The wet squelching sound would haunt me for days. Some of the blood splattered on me, but most of it flowed into the soil. He had become a man of bones and paper-thin skin, it was shocking to see that he still had so much blood.

All bright and red.

We carried his mutilated corpse to the open mass grave and threw it in. The disgusting stench of rotting flesh made me want to wretch, but I endured it to give Soon Ong's soul a Buddhist prayer.

"That's all nonsense you know. Illusions, fantasies, lies. There's nothing up there, nothing down below, nothing beyond," Yan Long said as we made our way to the camp.

"I need something to believe in," I croaked. My tone was almost pathetic.

Unexpectedly, Yan Long didn't have a snide retort, he just nodded. We rejoined the line and got back to work. Zi Han looked up at us and suddenly I remembered the words he said a few days ago. *Yan Long will kill you. He'll split your head open and all the bright red blood will seep into soil. It'll feed the trees.*

The realization shook me as it did Yan Long, we stared at Zi Han incredulously, but the boy just had a face of quiet acceptance. Then he spoke his next and ultimate prophecy.

"There will come a train that will take us far away from here. Far away from the pain and suffering. We will ride it to freedom."

* * *

Gradually, Yan Long and I accepted Zi Han's abilities of precognition. At first there was denial, some attempt at explaining the unexplainable, but the consistency and accuracy of his prophecies were simply undeniable. I used to consult a fortune teller back home for my business but he would always speak in vague generalities. In contrast, Zi Han's statements were precise and detailed. They were minor things, weather

10

changes, accidents on the line, times of Allied air raids, but whatever it was, every word out of his mouth was the inevitable truth.

Was he touched by the gods? Possessed by spirits or demons? We didn't know. Zi Han didn't know either, he described his visions of the future drifting in and out of his mind like old vivid memories. They came without rhyme or reason and he could only accept and absorb them. Eventually, we stopped caring about their origins and focused on what it gave us, certainty.

About two weeks after Soon Ong's death, our party sat outside the tents ready to dig into our dinners. It was the same meal every evening, a disgusting stodge of wet rice with a sprinkling of beans and peanuts, but for our tired broken bodies it was enough. I was just about to hungrily wolf it down when Zi Han suddenly grabbed my spoon and threw it away.

"What the hell?!" I said in shock.

"Don't eat that!" Zi Han commanded. Yan Long looked at him in confusion, but set down his spoon too. "It's infected."

"Infected with what?" Yan Long asked.

"Cholera."

Blood drained from my face and a chill ran down my spine. Malaria, beri-beri, dysentery, jungle rot, there were many diseases that plagued the camps, but all paled to the ravenous demon that was cholera.

"I see a vision of the camp a few weeks from now. The clatter of the rail will fall into a ghostly silence, the only sounds I hear are the moans of hundreds of men lying down in the mud begging for release. The flies salivate as they flock around the dying. Mountains of bodies are piled and burned in never ending fires. The air becomes so thick with black smoke, some of the sick die choking."

Zi Han had the same strange cold tone when he told us all

this. I was shaken by his apocalyptic glimpse of the future. It took a moment to truly process it, but after I did, I did not hesitate. I dumped the food and Yan Long and Zi Han followed suit.

The rest of the party noticed our actions and looked at us incredulously. Arif approached me and asked "Something wrong, brother? Why aren't you eating?"

"The rice has been infected with cholera, don't eat it. None of you eat your rice, it's got cholera!" I shouted in Malay to the party. Chatter and confusion spread throughout the men, but they all stopped eating.

"Why did you tell them that?" Yan Long whispered to me in Chinese.

"Are you stupid, Yan Long? We're all crammed in that tiny tent, we don't even have latrines for heaven's sake! If they die, we die!" I snapped back.

"What do you mean cholera? How do you know this?" Arif asked.

I blanked out, unsure how to respond. I couldn't exactly tell them that Zi Han had the power of clairvoyance. "Just believe me, please. If you eat the rice, you'll die, we'll all die," I pleaded looking into his eyes. Arif met my gaze and stared at me for a while, then he moved over to dump his food.

"You believe these guys, Arif?" said Nazir, another young Malay worker.

"I'm not taking chances."

"It's nonsense! We can't go without dinner! We'll be starving in our beds," Nazir responded.

"You'll have to do more than go without dinner. All the food in this camp has been contaminated, that means no breakfast or dinner tomorrow either," Zi Han said. As a new immigrant, his Malay was broken and choppy, but judging by their reactions they got the gist of it.

"What?! We'll die in a day working the line if we don't eat!"

Uproar and panic set about in the crowd, but Zi Han was unshaken, his boyish face was cold unyielding steel. "You'll have to suffer for the night and the next day as well, but I promise you, at the end, there will be a feast."

Zi Han began telling us what he saw, and what we had to do. We all listened, utterly enraptured by the conviction radiating in his voice. He was not telling a story, he was reciting history yet to unfold. All doubts melted away in the face of it. We went to bed with our bodies aching in hunger but our souls nourished in something we thought lost long ago.

* * *

Every morning, we were marched to our work stations. It was a long long walk that made me dread the endless drudgery that awaited, but I was accustomed to it, that dread was an old familiar friend. But today, the dread I felt was an entirely new beast, my nerves were an utter wreck. When we passed through the railway line and all the other workers slaving away, my eyes were wide open, darting around in fear and anxiety.

"Bodhisattva Guanyin, Goddess of Mercy, look over us," I prayed and prayed and prayed for success.

When the railway spike that was silently passed up the line finally landed in my hands, I breathed a sigh of deep relief. Gaurav, a light-fingered Indian worker in our party, managed to smuggle away a spike just like Zi Han said he would.

I handed the spike to Zi Han and he quietly kept it in his palm. We were further from the railway line now, walking on a small dirt road that led us to a forest where we were assigned to chop down lumber for bridges and huts. Just as we were about to enter the forest, Zi Han quickly knelt down to plant the spike on the road.

It was done, and now we just had to wait.

Wait and believe.

"That's it?" Arif asked, pointing discreetly at a huge misshapen tree with an ominously dark hollow trunk, big enough for two little children to hide in.

"That's the one," Zi Han affirmed.

We set about working, the ax felt heavier in my arms than usual, each swing at the trees brought me closer and closer to the brink of collapse, but I endured. We all crushed the hunger and pain inside us while the Japanese officer just watched us in boredom. To him, this was just another day. When the sun began to retreat, he yelled at us to stop, pack up, and leave.

Back on the dirt road, my hands started shaking in nervous anticipation. When I heard the whir of the truck's engine coming behind me, I closed my eyes for a second. All day, my mind conjured up visions of what would happen based on Zi Han's words and it happened exactly as my mind pictured, exactly as he said it would.

The truck passed us and sped forward before its left tire burst. It sped out of control, veering off the road and slamming against a tree. The sound of metal crunching against wood was satisfying bliss.

The Japanese officer looked on in shock while we all remained stoic and placid. He rushed to his comrades in the truck. They were still conscious but squinted and staggered out in disorientation. We all crowded forward to look, feigning interest. In truth, we purposely obscured the distracted Japanese officers from what was currently occurring on the back of the truck. Arif had snuck atop and was passing two crates down to Nazir and Yan Long. Two crates were what Zi Han had visioned them taking, so, that was what they did. I was no longer nervous. In fact, I had to stifle down a joyous laugh when I glimpsed at Nazir and Yan Long slinking off into the forest.

* * *

That night, when Nazir and Yan Long snuck back into camp with their arms full of the bounty, the tent was filled with such glee and excitement I was afraid the guards would be alerted. We marveled at what was collected, food supplies for the Japanese, cans of beans, peaches, pineapples, taros, sweet potatoes and even tuna.

As Zi Han promised we would, we feasted.

Well, sort of, as heavenly as the simple assortment tasted on our impoverished tongues, we had to ration it for the next few days. More importantly, Zi Han said we would need to save the supplies for 'the escape.'

The word sent chills down my spine.

Yan Long and Nazir weren't able to bring all the food back with them to the tent. Most of it was stashed in the large hollow tree near where we cut down lumber. So for the next few days, each of us would sneak off one by one to the tree hollow and smuggle a can or a packet of food back to camp. We worked together keeping watch of the oblivious Japanese officers.

Eventually, Zi Han's prophecy came true and the entire camp became ravaged with cholera. Hundreds of workers around us started dying, the nights were filled with echoes of their anguished moans, the days would consist of walking over corpses lying openly on the line. The Japanese medics came to our little tent wrapped up in their skin-tight gloves and face masks to inspect us. They found our small party was the only one entirely uninfected by the disease, a true miracle. Wary of losing more men, we were sent farther north of the camp, a little farther from this primordial plague with cleaner conditions and safer food.

Unfortunately, the Japanese forced us to do almost double the work to make up for the lost workforce. The officers bashed their batons on us if we weren't fast enough and only released us when the darkness of night made it impossible to continue. It was a miracle we didn't die from the endless grind.

Actually, it wasn't a miracle at all.

We preserved because Zi Han told us we would live, that a train was ready to take us to freedom.

We discussed this promised train at length, the entire railway line wasn't finished yet, but certain sections of it were already operational with the Japanese sending freight trains up and down in their haste to end the Burma conflict. Zi Han told us that in two months' time, our section would be functional and trains would be slowly limping across the rails. It seemed impossible but the Japanese had already brought more laborers and prisoners up north to replace the dead and with the way they worked us to the bone, it wasn't too surprising.

A train would come and take us south back to Malaya.

But escaping by train was not the difficult part, we would have to alight it eventually at checkpoints, the true gauntlet was surviving the jungle, the wild animals, the raging rivers, steep hills, and deadly ravines. There had been many attempts before us. When I first arrived, I witnessed the aftermath of one such attempt.

Seven Tamil workers escaped into the jungles and what greeted them was almost as horrible as the camps. They spent weeks wandering the savage wilds until there were only three of them left. Eventually, they found a remote Siamese village, but the village chief feared repercussions and informed the Japanese of their presence. They were brought back to the camp, and I witnessed their execution. They didn't make a sound when they were shot, their bodies just fell limp onto the dirt like dolls.

Their spirits were already gone long ago.

But they didn't have Zi Han. We had two months to prepare and plan our escape with all the necessary information. He didn't lay it all out at once, visions came to him slowly in bits and pieces, day by day. Under his guidance, we gathered what we needed. He told us where and when we could steal kits from the Japanese, which British prisoner was willing to trade his compass, where to stash all our supplies.

Out on the line, our party of Malayans slaved away together, and in this task we were truly united. We all had our roles to play in the escape. Gaurav's quick fingers were essential for stealing supplies, Muthu's drawing skills helped us sketch out a detailed map, Dinesh's knowledge on traditional Indian medicine would be vital in combating diseases, Arif's charm disarmed hostile Japanese officers, Karthi's talent in hunting would help us tame the wilds, and on and on it went. Even someone like me had use, my business managerial skills helped with the logistics and overall planning.

Before, we were just strangers sleeping under the same tent, but now I learned all the names of the people in our party, heard all their stories. Kamal and Chandran told us about how the Japanese came and rounded them up like cattle at the rubber estate where they had once worked like dogs for the British. Arif told us about how the Japanese locked up the doors of his village mosque during the Friday afternoon prayer, and demanded all the young men give themselves to the Japanese empire. His father begged for them to take him instead of Arif, but they just smashed a rifle against his head.

Yan Long was surprised by how similar the stories were to our own.

As the days went by, the confidence in our escape plan only

grew stronger. It wasn't just the progress we were making, but the fact that Zi Han's predictions became increasingly detailed and precise. We knew which routes to take, which village was occupied with the Japanese, even what animals would fall into our traps. He no longer had to wait for the visions, he could summon them. We would ask Zi Han questions about the situation and he would answer us immediately.

One day, Yan Long asked him a question, the one for which we all had been dying to know the answer. "When will The War end?"

Zi Han took a deep breath and closed his eyes. When he opened them again, he had the familiar glassy look. "The war ends in August, 1945. The end will come in the form of two brothers formed from splitting the core of reality. They erupt in a flash so bright it burns my eyes. A tree of smoke and fury rises in its wake, towering over the entire world. Two Japanese cities are shattered in an instant. The Japanese surrender. The Empire is no more."

A cheer went round the tent when he finished. I felt my entire body float in peace for the first time in months. There was an end. It was two years away, but it would come.

"Those dirty Japanese dogs will get what's coming to them!" Yan Long said with glee. Everyone excitedly discussed the end of the war and the Japanese defeat, but Zi Han's face was not one of celebration, it was somber and drained of all color. I noticed he was actually shaking. I asked him what was wrong, but he just looked at me with a haunted gaze and remained silent.

Zi Han's powers of precognition had become so great he began seeing visions of events twenty years in the future then fifty then a hundred. He entertained us with stories of a future where almost everyone had their own cars to drive, then a future where the cars drove us! He spoke of mankind leaving the earth and making its first step on the shores of the moon, the worst diseases of our times being driven to extinction, and an independent Malaya free from colonial rule for the first time in centuries.

When he mentioned the red wave of communism engulfing both China and Eastern Europe, Yan Long almost jumped in joy. He asked Zi Han if communism would take Malaya. Zi Han only said, "For a period."

People began asking Zi Han questions about their own futures or the well-being of their families. They always left with answers that gave them big, happy smiles, yet Zi Han looked strangely morose after relaying each fortune. I became very worried for him, while we grew stronger with hope each day, Zi Han's already skeletal frame grew even more gaunt and brittle. He was always a quiet one before, but now he seemed lost in his sea of visions. That cold listless look had become his default expression. Still, he kept brushing me aside and saying he was fine.

We were eating dinner outside the tent one day when Arif finally summoned the courage to ask a question, the answer to which he had been dreading.

"Is my father well, Zi Han? I didn't see what happened to him after they took me away and..." he choked up before he could complete his sentence.

"He's in good shape. He misses you, but he is well. There was no lasting damage from the knock on his head," Zi Han responded.

Tears started streaming down his face "T-Thank you, Zi Han. Thank you!"

Arif embraced Zi Han in warm gratitude and then walked away to collect his emotions. When he was out of sight, Zi Han's shoulders slumped down despondently and he sat limply like a husk drained of life.

"Hey, you okay, Zi Han?" I asked.

Zi Han looked at me with a tired smile and said "You never ask me any questions, Foo Xian. Don't you want to know your future or that of your wife and child?"

"I don't know, maybe deep inside I'm too afraid to know, but I think it'll be better if I find out for myself. Gives me something to look forward to."

"You don't think something bad is waiting for you?"

"I consider it, but I think my fortune is turning, the bodhisattvas are looking after me and my family. They brought you into my life after all, into all our lives to save us."

"You sound so ridiculous. Always putting your faith in these imaginary gods," Yan Long said, appearing suddenly beside us.

"Gods or no gods. I choose to believe in hope," I responded.

Zi Han gave a weak smile and said, "It's good you have a choice."

"What do you mean?" I asked.

He took a long pause, the familiar distant look dominated his face again. "I see things now. All kinds of things. The good and the bad. Things I don't want to see. I don't have a choice but to see. Things I don't want you all to know."

"Are you saying you're lying to us?" Yan Long asked.

"No, not lies. More like omissions. Half-truths," Zi Han answered. He took another long pause before he looked at us again. "Like what I told Arif. It's true that his father is well now, but in two year's time, he won't be. After the Japanese fall and before the British return, the communist takeover large swaths of Malaya and they go around reaping their vengeance against the 'collaborators.' Arif's father is deemed one of them, as are many Malay village chiefs. The communist put a bullet in his head at the very same spot where the Japanese rifle hit him so many years ago."

Yan Long looked at Zi Han in shock and disbelief for a moment, then his face turned to stone. "Well, he must have done something to deserve that then."

"How can you say that, Yan Long?!" I snapped in anger. "You worked with Arif, you know him well enough by now. You know that none of these people are the caricatures you imagine them to be. They are real living human beings."

"All traitors deserve death!" Yan Long said so loud he practically shouted.

"Your heart is as black and cruel as the Japanese soldiers. You're not so different from them."

Yan Long's face became flushed with red hot rage, I could see the veins of his forehead bulging. For a moment, I feared he was going to strike me, but he turned away and stalked off.

"See. There are things you don't want to know. Knowledge that only brings suffering," Zi Han said. He walked off too, to who knows where, leaving me all alone.

* * *

It was another night without rest, I prayed even more than usual for the safety of my wife and child. The mantra cycled in and out endlessly through my mind. Just a while more and I'll see them. I'll hold them in my arms and never let go, but seeds of doubt were growing inside me. What if nothing awaited me back home? What if I no longer had a home to go back to? I could do nothing but pray. I had to believe these prayers were churning the wheels of karma, that I had some small ounce of control.

In the darkness of the tent, I heard slight ruffling and saw the familiar shape of Yan Long. I thought he was prepared to recite his own mantra of death, but instead he rose up and left the tent. Somehow the loneliness of his dark silhouette compelled me to follow him.

Outside, the moon hung on the sky like a mirror. Under its silver light, I saw Yan Long more clearly along with the glinting blade of his knife. He held the knife he adored so much close to his face and studied it closely like it held some secret message.

"What do you want?" he asked, not turning to face me, eyes still on the knife.

"To apologize. I'm sorry for what I said," I said sincerely.

"You meant what you said and I meant what I said. All traitors deserve death. I deserve death."

"What do you mean?" I asked in confusion.

Yan Long put the blade down and stared off into the distance, far into the darkness of the jungle.

"My unit planned an ambush on a Japanese patrol. We thought it would be an easy job, but it was a trap. They lured us in and we were outnumbered and outflanked. It wasn't a battle, it was a massacre. All my comrades died bloody violent deaths, and I did nothing to stop it."

"Like you said, Yan Long, you were outnumbered. You couldn't..."

"There was a moment where we could have retreated. I was supposed to provide cover for my captain. He was like an older brother to me, he turned me from a scared little farmer into something more. I saw the soldier pointing the gun at him, had him in my sights, but I didn't pull the trigger. It wasn't that I froze up. I had killed plenty of times, I knew how to. I was in control. It was a conscious choice I made not to shoot. My captain's head burst into bloody pieces like a squeezed orange. I hid just like I did when the Japanese massacred my village. When the soldiers found me, I sobbed and begged like a pathetic coward. All insurgents are supposed to be executed immediately, but for some reason the Sergeant didn't do that.

He pitied me. Gave me mercy and shipped me here. I should have died. I deserve it."

I absorbed Yan Long's confession and looked at his figure, the shape of him illuminated by moonlight. I was suddenly struck by how young he was. He was hard, resilient, so full of life and rage that I forget he was just two years older than Zi Han. He was just a boy. All of them were just boys.

"No, Yan Long, you don't. You were saved and you're here now to live, to help in our escape. You're here to do good."

"That was what I told myself the first time I survived. I thought I was spared for a purpose, to fight the Japanese, and avenge my family, my neighbors, my people, but I failed at that. I failed my comrades."

I searched desperately for words to respond to him, but emptiness was all I had to offer. Yan Long took in this silence, his hands gripped the handle of his knife hard. Then, he passed me and returned into the shadows of the tent.

I remained outside for a while, the cold night air pierced my bones. I shivered while I kept on searching for words, the right words, the words I should have said, the words that could have soothed Yan Long's poor troubled soul. I had nothing. I felt utterly helpless. So, I went back to bed and prayed. For the first time, I didn't pray for my family, but for Yan Long and all the other lost young boys beside me.

* * *

The day of our escape drew closer and closer, and Zi Han became weaker and weaker. He turned into a living corpse, eyes cold and dead, lips pale and bloodless. When he worked the line with us, we watched him closely, fearing he would collapse at any moment. If he was lost in a fog of visions before, now he was drowned in an ocean of them. Most of the time, Zi

Han muttered to himself unintelligibly and ignored us like a man sick of mind. We tried taking care of him, stealing medicine, making herbs, but nothing worked. His sickness was as mysterious and otherworldly as his abilities. We could only helplessly watch him deteriorate.

Finally, the night came, the night of the train and the escape. We had everything we needed, all the stolen supplies and makeshift survival kits. Everyone was ready to go, everyone but the man who orchestrated this, Zi Han. He lay down inside the tent, too sickly to even move. I was reminded of the cholera victims, fading in the border of life and death out on the tracks. He was sweating and muttering in a feverish dream, but when Arif and I attempted to lift him up, his eyes snapped open.

"No... don't take me. Leave me," he commanded in a weak raspy voice.

"C'mon, Zi Han. It's time. It's what we've all been waiting for. We have to go. Please," I begged. The entire party was gathered around behind us, watching closely, adrift in uncertainty. For the first time in a long time, we were left without guidance. We were a ship about to set sail without our captain.

Zi Han looked at me. For the first time in ages, his eyes were clear and alive, but they were also pools of deep dark sorrow. "I saw my mother die. She was resistant when one of the soldiers at the comfort station came for her. So, he kicked her in the head. He kept kicking and kicking and kicking and kicking..."

Tears flowed down Zi Han's hollowed cheeks and I could do nothing but blubber, "I-I'm s-sorry." Again, I searched for more words, but again all I had was emptiness.

"I see my sister too. She lives through the war. She lives till old age, but she never recovers. I see her old and alone thrashing in her sleep, never finding peace, forever haunted by the horrors she endured. I see her dying all alone, in an empty house with no one around her. The neighbor's won't even find her body until the stench drifts over."

"That won't happen! You'll come with us and we'll find her. You'll be by her side and..."

"It doesn't matter, Foo Xian. None of this matters. I see the world a hundred years from now, a world engulfed in war, a war even bigger and more terrible than the one we are in now. Cities are turned to ash, people are consumed in an inferno of flames or die in slow agony from poisoned bodies. Then comes a winter that lasts forever. Darkness takes over the world. All life dies. In the end, the world is nothing but a sad lifeless husk."

I was too stunned to speak. All Zi Han's predictions had come true. So, this one must too.The ultimate fate of the world was war and death. It was too bleak for my mind to comprehend.

Zi Han looked at me with pity.

"I'm sorry, I shouldn't have told you that. Go, Foo Xian, leave me and go to your wife and child. Try to forget what I said and live your life. It's a good one, you'll be happy. I promise."

"I can't leave you. We won't."

"You have to. Remember what I said about half-truth and omissions. When I saw the vision, the vision of the train, I saw everyone boarding it except me and Yan Long. Not all of us get to escape."

I looked at Yan Long alarmed, but he just nodded peacefully at Zi Han.

"I'm sorry, but I'm dying here. I've known this for a while now," he said with a sad smile. His visions were truth, I could not refute them. I grasped his hands as hot tears filled my eyes.

"You're a saint. You saved us all. You'll be free of the

suffering of life, the cycle of reincarnation. You'll find peace in Nirvana."

"I-I don't want that...all I want is to see my sister and mother again."

"You'll get that Zi Han. They'll be with you in the next life."

Zi Han gave me another sad smile and said, "Tell me about this next life."

This time I did not need to search, the words flowed naturally into my mind and out of my mouth. I grasped Zi Han's hands even more tightly in mine, clinging onto his fading warmth.

"It's Chinese New Year's. You're driving down a road with your own car. You have a wife and child beside you. Both of them are pure and beautiful. You're going to visit your family. The road is full of other cars going home too. It is crowded beyond belief, but you wait patiently, you play games with your wife and child to pass the time. The sounds of joy bounce around in the car. Finally, you're there. You open the door and there's your family. Your mother, your sister, your father, they are all still your family in this life, too. They all smile at the sight of you, they are so happy to see you. You all sit down together to eat a big bowl of delicious hotpot. You catch up, talk, and laugh together. You are..."

I felt Zi Han's hands go limp in mine. Just like that, it turned cold. His eyes are closed shut. My brittle heart crumbled into ash. I started sobbing uncontrollably until I felt Yan Long's warm hand on my shoulder.

"I'm sorry, Foo Xian, but it's time. We have to go," he said compassionately.

I took in a deep breath, gathered myself, and looked at the rest of the party, faces disoriented with grief and confusion, but resolute in their determination to leave. I nodded and departed with them, careful not to turn back and look at Zi Han lest I break down again.

Just as Zi Han said, it was an unusually dark night, the air was stagnant and humid, heavy clouds pregnant with rain blocked the moon and stars. Under the cover of darkness, all nineteen of us sneaked off away from the camps and to the tracks undetected. When we finally arrived, I felt pulled out of reality. Even now in the distance, I could hear the sound of the train making its way down the tracks. I put my hand to the hard soil to feel the soft vibrations.

"Look! There are guards!" Nazir said, pointing at three Japanese soldiers patrolling idly along the rails. Strapped to their dark shadowy figures were the menacing blades of bayonets. We were still hidden among the trees, but there was wide open space between us and the tracks. It was a certainty we would be seen if we attempted to board the train.

"Zi Han never mentioned this!" said Kamal.

Suddenly, we could see the bright circular light of the train approaching. The rumbling of its engine grew louder. We bit our tongues in silence to help us remain undetected, but I could feel the panic striking through everyone.

"Zi Han said I wasn't coming aboard with you all. I have nobody to go home to anyway. I know what I have to do," said Yan Long. He pulled out his knife and took a step forward. He didn't say anything more, but he gave us one final look. In his eyes, I no longer saw rage and fury, but peaceful resolution.

Yan Long accepted his fate.

Fate.

Time slowed in that instance as I pondered it. The wheels of the train churned slower and slower until it melted into oblivion. Yan Long's fate was a sacrifice in death. Zi Han's sister's fate was a sad lonely death. The fate of the world was an ultimate apocalyptic death. All destinies Zi Han witnessed, future already pre-written. The tracks had already been laid down and all we could do was ride the train to the inevitable destinations.

But was this really true?

We all accepted Zi Han's prophecies as dogma, but we never challenged them. We never needed to, we floated with the tides because they were bringing us to shore. But beyond this shore was a deeper, darker ocean, with waves that will consume us as we wade in.

I wanted to swim.

I grabbed Yan Long's arm and said, "No. I'm doing this."

"W-What?!" he said in shock. "You have a wife and child, Foo Xian. Don't be foolish."

"And you'll take care of them, Yan Long. Just like you'll take care of Zi Han's sister. I know you will. Tell them.... Tell them that I prayed for them and I love them."

"No! Don't fight me on this! This is my atonement!"

"You deserve life, Yan Long. The world deserves life," I said. I put my arms around him in a warm embrace and gently took the knife from his hands. I dropped it on the ground and walked slowly out of the trees.

"YAMERU!!!" the Japanese officers shouted when they saw me. I stood still for a second while they cautiously approached me with their rifles drawn. I saw the train barreling forward and illuminating them with its golden light. Then, I bolted. I ran as fast as I could in another direction. They began shooting at me. The sounds of gunfire joined with the roar of the train into a chorus of chaos. But I was still too far, they all missed, and had no choice but to pursue me as I dashed into the darkness of the jungle.

I looked back and saw the officers chasing after me, huffing and panting while they aimed at me. Beyond that I saw my brothers run and climb aboard the moving train, lifting each other up atop it.

I smiled.

A bullet smashed into my shoulder.

Agony shot through me, but I continued running. Another bullet pierced my back and went clean through my flesh. Still, I continued running. I ran as blood began pouring out of the holes, out of my mouth. One last bang echoed in the forest, this bullet tore into the flesh and bone of my right leg. I could run no more and collapsed into the muddy forest floor.

The Japanese soldiers gathered around me, yelling in words I could not understand, but I ignored their voices and focused on the sounds of a train slowly fading away. As darkness consumed me, I prayed one last time. It wasn't for me or anyone, the mantra just brought me peace as I slipped into nothingness.

* * *

Atop the train, Yan Long stared in wonder at the Siamese landscape passing by. Here, the jungle no longer looked like an ominous hellscape but a dazzling paradise. He saw egrets gliding gracefully down sparkling rivers, ancient majestic trees bathed in morning light swaying with the wind. And he was spellbound by the beauty of the world.

While the train took them down south, Yan Long told Arif about Zi Han's vision of his father's death, how the communists will come to his village and execute him. However, Arif just listened to it calmly.

"Well, Foo Xian proved that Zi Han's predictions don't always come true. You told me and I'll make sure this doesn't happen," he said.

The thought that they had become untethered from the

future Zi Han had foresaw struck Yan Long with existential dread. Would they still make it out of Siam alive and back to Malaya? Is the fate of the world still the extinction of life? Or was that a foregone conclusion they were powerless to stop?

Yan Long put those thoughts aside for now and just enjoyed the wind rushing through his hair while the train kept rolling forward. He suddenly knew what he had to do to honor Zi Han and Foo Xian's deaths.

I'll make sure their souls will rest easy and be reborn in peace. I know they will. I chose to believe in Zi Han's prophecy. He said, There will come a train that will take us far away from here.

Far away from the pain and suffering.
We will ride it to freedom.

THE PEOPLE PLEASER

BY BRIANNA FERGUSON

Petunia Hartman was a kind soul, and you'd be wasting your time trying to prove otherwise. Had she ever wronged a single person who crossed her path, it was only in the dim, gray spaces of her childhood, where such a half-formed personality as that of a small child might allow for transgressions, one would balk at in a more solid state of being. For Petunia (fully grown, that is) there was no higher purpose in this life than to create harmony wherever one could. To get bent out of shape over the trips and travails of daily existence was to forget for a moment that life was short and everyone was suffering. Were she ever, for instance, to get cut off in traffic, or bumped back in a line-up for which she'd taken pains to arrive early, Petunia was adept at quashing whatever mammalian, under-evolved part of her brain took umbrage with such slights and converting the flood of outrage into something calm and sensible. Perhaps the person who cut her off in traffic was headed to the hospital to say goodbye to their beloved friend who'd seen them through thick and thin, and who was now expiring at such a rate that said cutter-offer might not make it in time to say their goodbyes.

Or perhaps the person budging in a line for the movie theater just received the news that that slight blurred vision they'd been experiencing of late was not due to monitor fatigue, but to a tumor the size of a baseball pressing down on their optic nerve. Perhaps, said tumor had occluded Petunia from their peripherals as they sought to enjoy what could easily be the last feature film of their life.

Oh, Petunia wasn't so highly evolved as to go about her days without experiencing even the littlest kick of indignity—she was, after all, a red-blooded human, the same as anyone else—but she liked to think she had enough wits to realize that giving voice to every little annoyance and devoting one's time and energy to exacting revenge was a waste of one's very finite time on this Earth. Not only that, but trying to right the perceived wrongs perpetrated against oneself tended not to yield the desired results, but to escalate the situation to an unnecessarily heightened dramatic state in which neither party walked away any better for the trouble.

And then there was the humiliation of apology. Whether giving or receiving an apology, it hardly mattered. The whole thing left her feeling sick and exposed.

No, thank you.

The world was unfair, and that was all there was to it. On a large scale, most people seemed to understand that. They understood that everyone they knew (including themselves) would age, sicken, and die—often far too early. They understood that it mattered very little how hard one tried at a particular task, or how naturally talented one might be in a particular arena, for when it came to reward and recognition for one's efforts, the world often looked the other way. But on the small scale—on the scale of stolen parking spaces and misplaced mail—people tended to think they could do something to establish peace and harmony by sticking their necks out. And to that simple pretense, Petunia simply couldn't agree. Life was far too short and far too fickle to spend one's precious time worrying about the unnecessary tithes Life seemed so eager to claim each day.

And so it was that Petunia made it through the first forty years of her life with a fraction of the scrapes and ills that plagued most of the people around her.

As a senior at the high school in the small town in which Petunia had lived her entire life, she became employed at a local Food 'n' Friends as a cashier. The more coveted jobs for people her age—the movie theater, the radio station, the summer boat rentals—all such places faced steep competition and low demand. But the Food 'n' Friends with its long hours standing in one place, its mostly aged, ornery, rather particular clientele, its unappealing hours and low pay was constantly in need of fresh blood. And so Petunia, always looking to pick up society's slack, applied and was instantly hired as a cashier. Oh, the manager would have loved to pay her the mandatory minimum wage from the get-go, but as Petunia was still a minor (and an inexperienced one at that) the usual minimum wage laws didn't apply. And what would the other cashiers think who'd started off the same as Petunia if Wally (the daytime manager) were to pay her minimum wage from day one, while several of the others had been forced to work all through high school just to achieve that kind of pay?

Naturally, Petunia made no protest, and her wage was implemented at a good $2.50 below the minimum wage of the time.

After graduation, Petunia voiced a desire for university to both her parents and to Wally. Their responses were disheartening, but not unexpected. Her parents—hard-working, yet ignominious lifelong citizens of a town whose only claim to fame was the annual jellyfish spawn—informed her that there was no money for college, and anyone silly enough to shackle themselves to student loans at a mere seventeen years of age might as well sign up for a lifetime of slavery, because paying off student loans for the next fifteen or twenty years would be very much the same as that. And what if something were to happen to her? How would she feel leaving her parents with such a debt (student loans were hereditary, after all) when they could barely make ends meet as it was? And what about poor Wally—did she have any idea what kind of a bind she'd be leaving him in if she were to leave in September, JUST when all the other high school employees went back to school? She was the most reliable cashier they had. If she left, it wasn't ridiculous to conjecture that the whole store might go belly up within the month.

Of course, Petunia relented, and retained her position.

And what of the mailman who came in every morning (he said) just to see her? Paul was his name, and he was what you might call a member of the dregs of society. Already thirty-five years old to her seventeen, Paul came every morning for a cold coffee and a sticky bun from the bakery, and he always insisted on going through Petunia's checkout line, regardless of whether she was on a regular line, or the express line for which his meager daily order would have been entirely appropriate.

At around five foot ten, and skinny as a lamp post, Paul had watery eyes, a receding hairline, and halitosis that Petunia could detect even from the five or so feet the cash register/debit machine/scanner placed between her and the customers. Though never without a compliment for Petunia (usually something about her butt, which she was forced, on a few occasions, to point out was invisible in such a face-to-face engagement), Paul's daily repartee tended towards the weather, the government, and the declining moral standing of their country. Were she a more outspoken individual, Petunia might have remarked on several occasions that no, she DIDN'T believe immigrants were behind the rapidly climbing median temperature of the world, and no, she had never once worried that the government might be inserting microscopic monitors into her Cheerios. Yet Petunia, ever the understanding type, decided from day one to chalk Paul's comments up to the unfortunate side effects of a somewhat insular lifestyle (forced upon him, no doubt, by his rather unfortunate physique and limited economic means) and so, such opinions were not his fault, but something he was unfortunate enough to have to suffer through, like all those who had to listen to them every day (namely, herself).

When the proposal came, it was and it wasn't a shock to her. He'd been coming to her till every day for two years, and she'd even accompanied him on not one, but five dinner dates outside the limits of the Food 'n' Friends. Although she had imagined from time to time that the man she would one day marry might be handsome, financially solvent, and cogent enough to assume that a Food 'n' Friends checkout line might be inappropriate for something so grand as a proposal of marriage, Petunia immediately recalibrated her expectations the moment she saw the ring box sitting on the conveyor beside Paul's morning sticky bun and leaking coffee.

"Is this...?" she asked.

But Paul, who had unfortunately dropped his sweaty, wadded-up five-dollar bill onto the floor the very moment Petunia picked up the ring, was nowhere to be seen. By the time he straightened back up, though, Petunia had put two and two together as to what Paul's intention had been, and (to spare him any embarrassment over the dropped fiver snafu) she'd placed the ring on the required finger and arranged her face into an excited, surprised mask of acceptance.

Their wedding night was underwhelming, to say the least, but Petunia raised no complaint. To have done so would have been to attack her new husband in his most vulnerable egotistical arena, and that was something she simply would not do. Men, after all, were invariably insecure about their sexual prowess, and Petunia would not establish herself on her first night of marriage as the kind of wife who henpecked her husband into becoming an insecure, stoop-shouldered shadow of his former self. Sure, Paul might have spent next to no time tending to the less obvious (yet equally important) erogenous parts of her body, preferring instead to jump right to the main event (and its near-immediate completion), but Petunia decided immediately that she would brook no argument, and that the next time would be quite different (somehow, all on its own).

Although of course it was not.

The house in which Paul (and now Petunia) lived was a cramped split-level structure with the faint odor of cat litter (though neither of them had cats) and the not so faint odor of cigarette smoke, left over from Paul's mother who'd bequeathed the house to her only son (by default of having no will) upon her own expiration.

Their married life was not unpleasant, and the years passed quickly.

Although Paul insisted on near-nightly connubial unions, Petunia failed to conceive a child. Paul raised the topic from time to time, exhibiting a passion he rarely exhibited in other areas of their shared life (sometimes going so far as to accuse his wife of employing a clandestine method of contraception undetectable by his senses) but no such contraceptive ever proved extant, and by the time Paul expired in a tragic head-on collision between his mail truck and a UPS van both vying for the same exit, Petunia, at forty years of age, remained childless.

Still working at the Food 'n' Friends, Petunia's coworkers threw a wee wake for the now middle-aged cashier's departed beau. Although the majority of her colleagues were below the voting age (it being summer when Paul's van was crushed), the wake was (Petunia was forced to admit) a thoughtful gesture. Though not one, but five different people told her they would deeply miss "Pat," Petunia shrugged off the mis-step, relegating it to the rank of slights not worth pursuing. Indeed, she managed to maintain a grateful smile, tinged with tragedy through the entire proceeding.

That was, until her colleague of seven years (and one of the only other legal adults at the shindig), Jenny Marks, approached her and confessed that she and Paul had carried on together for a whole summer only a couple years before. The secret had been destroying her ever since, Jenny gushed, and she could hardly wait to unburden herself to Petunia who—she'd noted over the years—was one of the kindest, most forgiving souls on the planet. "I don't know how I could have done that," Jenny confessed, "but I'm so glad it's out there, and we can finally move on."

Although Paul had never quite reached that most secretive and penultimate place in Petunia's heart—the part where she couldn't hide behind even her desire to please—he had still been her daily companion these last twenty some-odd years, and Petunia was not above the impulses of instinct.

Seizing upon Jenny's smock, Petunia glowered at her colleague as she lifted her hand high into the air in a dramatic gesture that could only end in a satisfying slap across Jenny's pale, hardly contrite cheek.

Yet the hand froze in place before it could ever make contact. Not by any will of Petunia's, mind you, but by the surprisingly firm grip of Wally, her pallid manager who'd never (to her knowledge) shown such strength of resolve in all the years she'd known him.

After being so unceremoniously tossed from her own husband's wake (and, she assumed, from her long-standing position), Petunia found herself without a job, without a husband, and without the satisfaction of a good slap across the face of the woman who'd cuckolded her for God-only-knew how long. With financial ruin on the horizon, the only thing to do was to put the house on the market. Oh, Petunia begged Wally to take her back at the Food 'n' Friends once the excitement of a near altercation had settled down—after all, she had no education and no experience beyond her cashier job—but Wally had declined. He could not, he claimed, allow such a dangerous, unpredictably violent woman through his doors ever again. At least, not in the capacity of "employee."

And so, Petunia—at the end of her rope—called the only real estate agency that would drive the sixty kilometers from the next city over to help her sell her house.

The realtor, a sallow little woman named Louise with obnoxiously red hair (a bottle job, Petunia couldn't help noticing, but could DEFINITELY help mentioning) said the house would have to be let go at a few grand below market value, due to the damage from cigarette smoke, and the lackluster job market in such a dead-end town.

Would Petunia mind? The woman asked.

Petunia made a show of being so perfectly fine with the suggestion, it might have been her idea all along. But of COURSE, she would mind! Undercutting the house's value by thousands of dollars would leave her with almost nothing to pay off the remaining mortgage—let alone to put down a deposit on some place new. Petunia was just about to say as much, when she noticed the streaks of black marker on Louise's boots. The woman had clearly tried to fill in the peeled patches of her faux leather boots with a Sharpie, and the sight of it made Petunia sick. If the woman had so little money that she couldn't afford new boots, and if she was driving over a hundred kilometers round trip just to have a look at Petunia's house, then didn't Petunia sort of owe it to Louise to sell even if it meant taking such a huge loss?

"So, where are you headed now?" Louise asked two weeks later as Petunia shook hands with her realtor one final time and headed down the driveway with a box in her arms towards her idling car.

"Ohh, not too sure at the moment," Petunia confessed as she laid the box in her already over-packed trunk. "Couldn't really find anything satisfactory in time, so I suppose I'll just park somewhere for the night and figure things out in the morning."

Louise blinked hard and locked eyes with Petunia.

"Surely, you're kidding."

Petunia shrugged dramatically, as if to say "no worries, I'll take the next one," to someone sliding into the cab she'd just hailed.

If Louise ever found a response to Petunia's pitiable shrug, Petunia didn't hear it. Soon, she was in her car, speeding off to...to...well, she didn't know where to just yet, but she was sure she'd think of something.

It was 4:00am when she heard a rapping on her window. Rousing herself from the particularly uncomfortable slumber a car's front seat always managed to offer up, Petunia wriggled out from under her blanket, rolled down the window and looked up into the flashlight and consternated gaze of Wally. Doubling as both day manager and night security (since none of the other employees were either legal age or interested), he had not slept a full night in close to three years. Staring down through haggard, twice-bagged eyes, Wally looked less like an authority figure and more like a fellow parking lot tenant out sleepwalking.

"You'll have to move along," he said. "No overnight parking on private property." He'd failed to use her Christian name, and Petunia wasn't altogether sure that Wally had registered it was indeed her trying to nab a few winks before dawn.

"Wally, it's me," she said, unsure whether the familiarity would soften or harden his response. "It's Petunia."

Wally jerked upright and rubbed his eyes.

"Petunia! I didn't recognize you without your smock. What are you doing sleeping in your car?"

"I uh...I sold Paul's old place and I couldn't find anywhere else to stay in time."

Wally cocked an eyebrow, as if to say "that's the stupidest damn thing I ever heard," but he did little else besides pinch a damp bulb of snot from the tip of his nose and wipe it on his security man's jacket.

"Well, I'm awful sorry about your predicament, but like I say, you can't be spending the night here. Owner's don't want nobody on campus overnight."

"Wally," Petunia said, glancing over each shoulder in mock assessment of any potential listeners-in, "there's no one around. It's just you and me in this whole parking lot. Surely you can make an exception for the night."

"Sorry, P," Wally said. "I sure would love to, but the owners don't want nobody overnight. Say it lowers the value of the property."

Now Petunia really did look all around. Not only was the parking lot completely deserted, but the other parking lots nearby were also completely deserted, as was the highway that ran through the center of the town. Not since they'd begun speaking had even a single car driven by.

"Wally, there's no one around," Petunia continued, feeling an uncomfortable rush of blood to her cheeks. "And I know they don't have any security cameras out here...couldn't you just pretend you didn't see me and go about your business? I promise I'll be gone well before opening."

Wally looked down at his shoes—his shoulders (if possible) becoming even more slouched as he did so.

"I'm really sorry, Petunia, but rules is rules. Now, I'm real damn sorry, but you're gonna have to leave."

There was a ringing in Petunia's ears that would have made perfect sense were she stationed next to a jackhammer, or perhaps removing herself from the direct path of a jet engine. But she was simply sitting in her car, thinking of a way to get Wally to see the ridiculousness of the situation, and to let her stay.

"Look, Wally," she began, fighting to keep her voice steady. "I know it's your job to kick people out of the parking lot, but there's no one here but the two of us. There's no need for this exact parking space, or for any of the others. I'm sorry, but I'm not leaving. You can call a tow truck, but as they don't open until the store behind us here does, I doubt it will do much good. Now, if there's nothing else, I would very much like to get back to sleep."

With that, she rolled up the window, pulled her blanket high over her face, and closed her eyes.

For a minute or two, Wally lingered outside her door, offering up every "now, now" and "you'll be sorry" he could think of. After a few half-hearted jigglings of the door handle, though, he gave up and walked away.

Beneath the blanket, Petunia's heart thundered, beating out a song of triumph and liveliness against the purple cotton of her sweater. She had stood up for herself, and she had won! No messy hand-to-hand combat had broken out. No tears had been shed. Oh, there'd been a feeling or two—a little back and forth over who would come out on top—but in the end, she had gotten what she'd wanted. Never in all her life had she ever felt so alive! She could have leaped from her car and run laps around the parking lot, if she wasn't worried Wally was waiting for just such an opportunity to jump behind the wheel and steer her car to someplace less likely to land him on the receiving end of an unpleasant reminder about the responsibilities of Night Security Guard at the Food 'n' Friends off Route 6.

Though newly awakened as a being of agency and articulation, Petunia kept to her word, and was gone from the parking lot well before the first of the opening crew began to arrive.

With no other demands on her time (besides the trifling need for a house, an income, and somewhere to empty her bladder), Petunia made her way south to the beach, where the public restrooms and vast, empty parking lots would afford her some privacy in which to sort through her new world of possibilities.

The moment she was parked (in a good spot beneath a large tree with bushy, shady leaves—the kind of spot most people arrived early to claim, and which she would have normally felt awful about claiming for herself) Petunia extracted a notepad and a pencil from her glovebox, and began composing a list. There were so many ideas clattering about in her head, though, she could hardly get them down in a fashion that would prove readable later on.

What should she do first, now that she knew how to stand up for herself and TAKE what she wanted in this life?

A place to live was obviously at the top of the list. Rather than go crawling back to Louise, though, begging for help getting back her old house (which she'd secretly always hated), she planned to get a small cabin in the woods. Nothing fancy— just a single bedroom and space enough for...for...well, even if nothing came to mind just yet, SURELY plenty of passions were about to present themselves to her.

Maybe she'd become a painter!

With no fussy Paul fretting about the house, she'd be free to make any kind of a mess she wanted. And with no neighbors (not in the kind of cabin she was envisioning) she could play her music as loud and as late as she wanted! Oh, she had no idea what kind of music she'd play—never having delved too deeply into her personal tastes, before, lest they clash with those of someone else within earshot—but she would FIND her tastes, and listen to them as loud as she wanted.

And she'd get a career. Something they didn't want forty-year-old women to do. She'd march right up to the college admissions office and enroll in the longest, hardest, most expensive program she could think of. Debt be damned! Plenty of penniless people went to school, and as far as she could tell, most of them didn't wind up mumbling to themselves under a bridge. They wound up engineers, or lawyers, or both! There was nothing she couldn't do, now she'd begun to find her voice. By the time her turn came up to go quietly into the night, you could damn well bet there wouldn't be much quietness about it. Not with Petunia Hartman at the helm.

No sir, not ever again.

It was Sunday, though, and the college was closed. So, what else to do until then?

The ocean—which had always filled Petunia with a particular dread, due to its depth, its vastness, and its fondness for swallowing tepid swimmers whole—lay beautiful and blue before her, bathed in the glinting light of early morning. It was summer, and no doubt the water (for at least a few feet) was warm and very welcoming. Oh, there were signs everywhere warning of the jellyfish spawn, but Petunia paid them no heed. For she was not a woman of signs or warnings or rules, anymore. So, what if she kicked a jellyfish or two in the head in her struggle to stay afloat. Did the world really need one more breeding pair of jellyfish?

Ignoring every sensibility to public nudity laws, Petunia

shed her sweater, her pajama pants, and her shoes on the front seat of her car, and strode over the fifty or so yards of beach to the edge of the water with her head held high and proud.

From the shore, she couldn't detect any sign of jellyfish, but she hardly cared either way. If they were out there, they could damn well get out of her way. The last thing on God's green Earth Petunia Hartman was ever going to do was apologize to a bunch of stupid jellyfish.

A dipped toe confirmed that the water was every bit as warm as she'd suspected—perhaps even warmer. And wasn't that just the way of the new world? Stand up for what you want—reach out and take it—and it'll be better than you ever could have hoped.

By the time she was well and truly floating—bobbing in the water like a little brown (though rapidly graying) buoy— Petunia could feel the first silly fingers of the first curious jellyfish starting to tickle her toes.

"Excuse you," she muttered down at them, though it came out more like "Bl-blurp-bluh," owing to the water that rushed into her mouth as she tried to direct her words downward.

She kicked at one, and it sank down a few inches, but not before giving her a quick little jolt on the ankle.

"Ouch!" Petunia shouted, much clearer this time, as she jumped a few inches in the water. "That wasn't very poli—"

ZZZT

Another jolt sent shockwaves through her calf, nearly paralyzing the leg.

Petunia reached down to massage the immobilized digit as she eyed up the shoreline. The obviousness of her error was racing to overwhelm her, but she wouldn't let it.

Not today, of all days.

With her still un-paralyzed leg, she aimed a good kick out behind her as she paddled with both arms in the direction of the shore. That leg, too, however, made contact with the bulbous flesh of a jellyfish, and within seconds, both legs were fully paralyzed (not to mention, radiating with a blinding pain to which no other experience in Petunia's life bore any comparison).

Using only her arms, Petunia pulled herself towards the sandy line of the shore as best she could, but even with the fiery will of her new life coursing through her arms, there was simply too much dead weight beneath the surface.

This is what I get, she thought to herself as her head dipped below the waves. *This is what I get for taking a stand just once. The one goddamn time I try to do something I'm not supposed to, and—*

But no, it wasn't the one time. It was, in fact, the second time she'd disobeyed a posted sign (third, if you counted the beach nudity). The first time, of course, was the altercation in the parking lot of the Food 'n' Friends, and in that particular encounter, she'd come out well and truly on top, thank you very much.

As she sank deeper into the field of jellyfish, a triumphant smile still frozen (or paralyzed) on her face, the only thought in her silly little head was that she was definitely crushing more than just a single breeding pair of jellyfish...

...and she hoped she'd be forgiven.

VIRGIL IN KINGMAN

BY INBAL GILBOA

There's this road she takes, on the drive back from her sister's house, that doesn't look or feel like it was made to be driven on by the kind of human being she knows. It's not a bad road, by any means, but she doesn't like driving on highways, even at night, and it's the straightest path coming back and forth from her sister's place to her apartment, so she takes it.

It hasn't been paved in a long while, that's clear, and in her small car, the rattling of the asphalt makes her feel like her car is moments away from shaking itself apart.

The road is divided strangely - wide enough to be four lanes, like any good Arizona road, but actually being three - one right lane, one left, and the middle turning lane marked out with yellow lines. The two driving lanes are too wide, and the turning lane overtaking the single lane with every stoplight, and the driving lanes are both split down the middle where the asphalt cracked, so that it feels like your car is always tilted uneasily towards the shoulder of the road. To one side is a long concrete wall. To the other is open prairie.

The result of this is that, while the road is long and straight and easy, you can never relax your eyes while driving it, always staying at a medium consciousness of your surroundings, which makes the drive always feel much longer than twenty minutes. On the rare occasion where another car floats ahead of her, she can watch the driver slide their vehicle from one side of the wide lane to another, twitching and swaying like a bumblebee trying to get through a pane of glass. It was only in watching them bop around that she noticed herself doing it, trembling her little car from side to side along the road.

One could never truly relax on this road.

The fact that she had no recollection of picking up a hitch-hiker, despite there now being one in her car, did not help things.

He's sitting shotgun to her, not saying a word and certainly not wearing a mask, cloth or otherwise, just fiddling with the glove compartment, opening and closing it over and over again. Now, she's a proper Arizonan driver, in her little four-seater car, and she knows better than to acknowledge a passenger she has no memory of picking, so she ignores him.

She stops to refuel her tank at a Shell station outside of Scottsdale, tugging her mask on and tucking her hand sanitizer into her front pocket. She still has half a tank left, but she doesn't know how long it'll be before she comes back this way again, how long it'll be before she sees her brother and sister again, so she fills the tank back up all the way and leans against the car door as the clicking of the pouring gasoline sounds.

"Excuse me," she hears, from somewhere near her feet.

She glances down. A blonde, hoary tarantula is climbing over her shoe, and up onto her pant leg, in a slow, wobbly scale. "Good evening," she says.

"Hi," the spider replies. "Jacob Waltz, pleasure to make your acquaintance. Mind if I bothered you for yours?"

"Call me Sleeper Car," she says. She lowers a hand for him,

and Jacob Waltz climbs into the center of her palm, whereupon he continues to walk, letting her pass him from one hand to another, in a slow, conversational pace.

"Sleeper Car," he says. "Heading to the Underworld, are you?"

"How can you tell?"

Eight eyes grouped in two columns turn to the shotgun seat of her four-seater Hyundai, but Jacob Waltz does not acknowledge the passenger either. The hitchhiker, faceless and wordless, takes his phone out of his pocket and begins to pick at the touch screen without intent, uncomfortable.

She conceded the point. "Alright," she said, "where's the Underworld, then, Jacob Waltz?"

"Near Kingman, of course," he says, "where else? Across the Salt River."

She says, "The Salt River doesn't cross Kingman."

"Doesn't it?"

She thinks on it, and finds she's not so sure. It's not as though she's walked the length and breadth of the Gila and all its tributaries to see where each trail does and doesn't go. "Then I'll go to Kingman, and I'll cross the Salt River. And you're coming with me, Jacob Waltz."

"Of course I am," says Jacob Waltz, "it's a long way to the edge of the state, and you are in need of a guide."

"I have Waze on my phone," she says.

"Yeah, go ahead and type in *The Underworld* on Waze, Sleeper. No, go on. I'll wait."

Yielding the point, she places Jacob Waltz on her right shoulder to finish paying for her gas. Once she ducks back into the driver's seat, the tarantula ambles down the length of her arm, up the steering wheel, and settles at the dashboard, making himself comfortable there.

"And we're off," he says.

And they were.

* * *

By all accounts, she ought've been in Kingman hours ago.

If you check the map, it should only be about three hours to cross the state lines from Arizona to California, maybe four hours, maybe five. But she once tried to drive to California, in her little Hyundai, pushing hard against the desert winds, and once she saw the bloodied star of Arizona's state flag waving over the state lines, having spent a week weathering God, her engine had overheated, and she'd given up leaving then and there.

And she hates driving on highways, anyway. It's the way the road knows you're trying to race out of somewhere, and it has ways of punishing you for it.

It'll take them three days, Jacob Waltz says, maybe four, maybe five.

"Have you ever been to California?" she asks him, on account of her phone recharging and the radio stations being shit.

"Once," he says, "on the great ambling route that all male tarantulas make, coming down the mountain to celebrate before climbing back up the mountain to fuck prodigiously and die."

She says, "You seem very much alive."

Jacob Waltz seems humbled by that, and he makes a bashful turn about the dashboard. "Terribly alive, I am. In this lifetime, I've had twelve seasons, and the ground is full of my slings, hissing and throwing hairs as they should. But in twelve years, I've not known the pleasure of being killed by a lady I went courting, though I've lived it in previous lifespans."

"You'll have to forgive me for saying it, but I can't say the sound of being killed while fucking appeals to me very much, Jacob Waltz."

"That's on account of you not being a spider," he says, in a pitying tone, "to you, the air is quiet, and full of sand. You do not feel the vibrations of prey on the breeze, nor the magnetic pull of the mountain, to dance, to hunt, to kill, to die. I have lived a thousand years, crawling on the desert earth, and I will live a thousand more, for as long as there is desert earth to crawl on, all for the chance to once again live, and to live is to feed the person you love with your own body if you must. This is a language you will never speak."

She thinks on that, then she nods. "Fair enough."

They drive in silence. The night turns to a milky, purpling dawn. She intended on sleeping, but she doesn't feel tired at all. The desert warms up, hot and alive. God ascends on the world again, burning white hot on the horizon.

At a rest stop vending machine, she buys a bottle of water, a gun with three bullets, and an energy bar. She pays in a twenty-dollar bill, and the machine spits her change back to her, two dollars in quarters. She turns the coins on their side, and finds that one is a Wyoming quarter, the back printed with a simple, elegant design of a rider atop a bucking bronco. Running her thumb across the shining coin, the brilliant insignia, and thinks all at once that it is the most beautiful thing she's ever seen.

"Wyoming," she says, to herself more than anything.

"Never been," Jacob Waltz says. "I don't believe it exists."

"Yeah," she agrees, pouring her quarters into her pocket, like glittering little stones, like the precious teeth of a copper mine.

* * *

50

On the night of the first day, which they resolved to drive through, there's a monsoon. It's late August, the time of all times for a monsoon, and this one snarl and bites and kicks like a canyon mule, and they drive through it.

"It's a monsoon," she says, yanking the steering wheel hard against the wind. A storm like this would be hell in a truck, but in a little four-seater, it makes the bones of her skull tremble, mandible, maxillary, zygomatic, temporal.

Steady on the dashboard, Jacob Waltz insists, "It's a haboob."

He's been insisting that for the past hour, threatening that the storm will never break, explaining that this is the first layer of Hell, the howling winds of the undecided dead, who lived neither here nor there, who could neither help good or hinder bad, and so abided bad in quiet, indecisive ways. The road here is badly paved. Three times, in his lecture, he nearly shook all the way off the dashboard.

"It'll break," she says.

In the passenger seat, her hitchhiker murmurs something. Every time he opens his mouth, a thunder rolls in the mountains and drowns him out, but he keeps prodding at his phone unhappily, checking the weather, checking the news. He opens the glove box, compulsively palms at the emergency kit someone stored there, and nods to himself. She avoids making eye contact.

A truck passes them by, nearly running them off the road, and she just about cracks a tooth clenching her jaw. She reads the side of it as it moves past the window,

"GOD ENRICHES GOD ENRICHING GOD ENRICHED GOD"

then she turns her head back to the road.

God is nowhere to be seen. The cloud cover is too thick, and the air is hazy with red dust, the horizon a blurry orange, the road an Impressionist gray. "I hate highways," she says, to no-one. The passenger opens his mouth, and a crack of lightning tears the stomach of the sky open like a haruspex. It rains fat, slow-moving droplets.

"See?" she says. "I told you it's not a haboob."

Jacob Waltz only says, "There's something on the side of the road, there. There's someone. Sleeper, pull off the road."

She starts to say, "Nothing there," but her hands obey the instructions of the guide without her input, turning the steering wheel towards the shoulder of the road. There, as she takes her foot off the gas pedal and slows down in little pulses on the brakes so as to not grind them to ash, she sees the glinting shape of the motorcycle, the black heap of the motorcyclist, the three dirt-colored vultures hopping and shuffling in a circle around the motorcyclist, and she puts her car in park.

The motorcyclist is dead, of course. She hardly needs to get out into the sand and kneel in the mud to tell, her helmet was cast off in the crash and lies maybe a yard away from her body, her arms put out to either side like a Saguaro, her neck bent painfully to the side. One of the vultures comes near, and she kicks some dirt at it so it won't keep pecking at the corpse.

"Lovely animals, vultures," the corpse says. "They eat anthrax, you know?"

She thinks on that. "Like, for kicks?"

"No, they don't - they don't," the motorcyclist gets up on her elbows, her dead, fogged-over eyes coming to pinch holes somewhere on either side of Sleeper Car's shoulders. She's doing her best to make eye-contact, despite her broken neck, her face all scraped up with road rash. "They don't eat just the anthrax, they eat things that have anthrax in them, and then there's no anthrax anymore. They get rid of it. Say, would you help me up?"

In the hand that isn't scraped up to shit, the motorcyclist

has a tattoo of a playing card, the deuce of clubs. Even with her mask pinned up to her face against the wind, she can make it out when she gives the dead woman a hand up. Not knowing what to say, really, she settles on, "You're dead, in case you haven't noticed."

"I have noticed, yes," she says, "on account of the neck, you know. But I appreciate you making sure." After a moment, the motorcyclist seems to have caught enough control of her dazed eyes to look at the Hyundai, at the passenger seat and the dashboard. "Going to the Underworld?"

"I am," Sleeper Car says.

Casting a dithering look at her wrecked bike, she says, "Mind if I catch a ride? I don't think this one's taking me any further, and I need to get to the Salt River."

"To the Salt River? Yeah, I'll take you."

The dead motorcyclist tips her head in thanks, and then takes a moment to fumble with the backseat, since there's only a door on one side. She walks the long way around the front of the car, then goes ahead and takes a seat in the back.

"No mask?" Jacob Waltz asks, in lieu of a how-do-you-do.

"Ah," the dead woman says, very proud of herself, "can't catch COVID, already dead." and she taps the side of her nose twice with her index finger. "Name's Show Low."

"Show Low," Jacob Waltz repeats. "I'm Jacob Waltz, that's Sleeper Car. Do you speak any German, Show Low?"

"None," Show Low says.

"Goddamn. Whole state full of foreigners and none of them speak any German. Spanish?"

Show Low makes an excited sound, and then the two of them spend the next hour or two speaking in Spanish as Sleeper Car thunders down the highway. Eventually, her head starts to nod against the steering wheel, the passenger reaching out as if to shake her awake every time, but she startles and refuses to acknowledge him, or be acknowledged herself. This goes on until the sky turns a blue-black, speckled with stars you couldn't see in Phoenix, Cassiopeia in her chair and the Puppis of Argo Navis, and Jacob Waltz tells her she ought to pull aside to sleep, she ought to pull aside and find a rest area so they can all sleep, and they do.

* * *

In the morning, the monsoon is all gone, and so is the rest area.

It is the second day on the road, and instead of being on the road, she spends two precious hours of the morning searching all around them until she finds out that, based on the tracks and the location, a flash flood pulled their car in their sleep towards Winslow, far in the wrong direction.

"We're closer to Four Peaks than to Kingman," she says, which is probably an exaggeration. All along before them stretches out a yawning golf course, like the jaws of a green, artificial animal. She tries to take a step here and a step there and it all feels forbidden to her, the grass too young and green to be stepped on.

"You ever been to New Mexico?" Jacob Waltz asks, skittering across a rock pitiably. He's as confused about the change in scenery as she is.

Sleeper Car looks at him with a look of bald-faced offense so severe it could strip paint off a wall.

"Pardon," he says.

"I have!" Show Low says, delighted. Sometime over the night, she bandaged her wounded side in what remains of her tattered leather jacket, and righted her broken neck, but she remains no less dead. "I've been to New Mexico and Colorado, but it was hell and a half to get the paperwork to go to Colorado. Had to email the Mine Inspector, you know."

Jacob Waltz makes a disgusted sound. "Now there's a guy who belongs here."

An unrecognized number calls her just then, and when she checks her phone, it warns her that it's likely a teleprompter. She cancels the call as it comes and says, "I didn't vote for him."

"I didn't vote for him either," Show Low says, "well. I didn't vote for anyone. Thing is, I wanted to make an informed opinion, I wanted to research what I should do, and I did, but I just kept having late nights at work, and I never had the time, and then when I made up my mind, it was too late. I didn't vote for anyone."

Show Low looks appropriately bereaved about it. Above them, a small flock of red-eyed cowbirds, black and glinting like metal ingots, call to one another on the branches of an Ironwood tree.

"Uncanny, wouldn't you say?" Jacob Waltz says, cleaning the hairs of his eight legs one at a time.

"I wouldn't," she says.

"You wouldn't, Sleeper?"

She says, "I wouldn't say uncanny. It's not familiar enough to be that - uncanny lives in the private and intimate. It's a lover's shape, lying in your bedsheets, unrecognizable to you. That," she says, cupping a hand over her forehead to glare at the horizon against the harsh light of God, "is just fucking creepy. Where are we now?"

Looking at the red-eyed cowbirds, Jacob Waltz sighs and rolls his eyes, every hair on his hoary body prickling high and vicious. "These are the fields of the unrepentant, where the gluttonous souls of the living, who in their lives were parasites on their countrymen, and in their deaths, remain parasitic."

The dozen or so cowbirds above them sing at one another mercilessly, seeing only their competitors. The golf course is barren, without even the diesel-fuel smell of a lawn mower, or the bumping, rickety noise of golf carts bumbling along. It's only them, the cowbirds, and, after a moment of looking, three javelinas lying together in the shade of a tree, easily mistaken for rocks.

"Good morning," she says to the javelinas, out of politeness, who wake up one at a time, slow-moving in the cool morning and reluctant to rise. One yawns, revealing its cactus-eating tusks, its root-digging tusks, its coyote-goring tusks, and gets to its hooves with surprising elegance, its two siblings following in short order.

"What are you?" it asks.

"Who are you?" the second asks.

"Why are you?" the third asks.

She says, "Sleeper Car. I'm a driver. I'm here for the Underworld. You know the one."

The javelinas look at each other suspiciously, apparently not satisfied with an answer of that nature. Having come to a silent consensus, they say, "Why are you going to the Underworld? / What will you give to get there? / What will you take with you when you leave?"

Finding those questions not as easy as the first batch, she allows herself a minute to ponder that, but only a minute, because javelinas are javelinas, and these are beginning to snort and huff uneasily. "I am going to the Underworld to find something I forgot. To get there, I will give as much as I need to get there and return, no more and no less. When I leave, I intend to leave with a little more than I came in with."

These answers, the three javelinas like a little better, and they jostle each other heartily, ready to start the day. The third says, "Then go to Meteor Crater, and walk into the mouth of Hell. It should be no small feat, keeping your mask on, but you have plenty of practice, descending into the deeper layers."

Defensive, she demands, "How should I have that?"

Already on their way away, the javelinas hardly spare her a second glance as they wander off into the golf course, pausing only to say, "The deepest Hell is for the living, Sleeper. That, you should already know."

* * *

"Did you know there's a town in Arizona called Carefree?" Show Low says, as they ascend up the steps to Meteor Crater, to look down into the mouth of Hell. "Carefree and Surprise, I always liked that. There's a town called Santa Claus, too. An unincorporated community."

The mouth of Hell looks like a meteor impact site, with the accordion folds of where different epochs, whole different ages of the world, were pressed together and sealed shut by the heat and pressure of a meteor collision, sealed tight and timeless like an unopened envelope. At the core of it, Sleeper Car thinks she can see a massive animal, but she uses one of the telescopes littered around the top of the meteor site to look below and it's only the metal shape of a pump. The passenger, standing right behind her, fidgets without saying a word until she lets him have a look too.

He's very quiet, this passenger. She can't bring herself to look at the void across his head where a face should be, except in brief glances, but when she does, she can maybe see a pair of eyes clearing up. He's quiet, which is odd to her, even though she doesn't know him. In places like this, everything has to be quiet to be heard at all, the way her lover says her name all slow and safe in the mornings, like a red cardinal at a bird feeder sings to his girl, saying: *come eat, come eat, come eat.*

Show Low continues talking. "Isn't it strange that this place is called Meteor Crater? It ought to have a name, but it doesn't really, it's just named for what it is. They wanted to call it

Barringer Crater, originally, but they don't name meteor impact sites after people, they name them after landmarks, and well, there weren't any. They named it after the nearest post office, and the post office was named after the meteor crater, so, well. Meteor Crater the meteor crater. Funny."

She tries to look harder at the crater. Tries to find the seam between their world and the next, but can't. Everything folds together like welded layers of sediment, too hot and pressurized to split apart. Her phone rings and she answer the call without looking at it. It's a robot caller again, and as soon as she says, "Hello?" she can hear the call connecting.

"Hello?" the cheery recorded voice echoes. "Sleeper? Turn around. Turn around, Sleeper. Turn around."

Sweat runs down the nape of her neck. She disconnects the call and holds her phone in her hand. The background of her lockscreen is a picture of herself and someone she doesn't recognize, but his eyes seem familiar. They look happy together.

Jacob Waltz "Hey, what kind of phone is that?"

She says, "It's a 9S."

He says, "No such thing. It goes 8 Plus and then X. Don't you know that?"

She says, "Mmhm. Hold on just a minute," then she winds her arm back as far as it'll go and she throws her phone into the mouth of Hell.

Show Low says, "Lots of unincorporated communities in Arizona with fun names, you know. There's one called Rare Metals, there's another called Three Way, and one called Boneyard. There's a town called Hope. There's a town called Why. There's a town called God, Forgive Me. There's a town called Please Forgive Me. There's a town called, God, Please Forgive Me."

* * *

After the Meteor Crater, they drive for another three, four, five hours, until God settles in the middle of the sky, so hot and burning that they're all yawning in their seats, exhausted by the harsh light. There is a physical exhaustion to it, to being in the light for so long, like plants wilting. She wishes she was a Saguaro now, big and amiable, with a barrel chest filled with water. Unyielding.

At four in the afternoon, a sand storm picks up. By five, visibility is so poor that they have to drive with their high beams on. By six, the light is starting to diminish, and even the high beams can't help them, so she pulls off to the side of the road to wait it out. The car warning system complains incessantly that the two front tires are depressurized, and she sighs, and resigns herself to going to check on them, despite knowing it's only the air pressure from the weather front causing the differentials.

She gets out of the car and checks the tires, seeing that they are as perfectly filled as always, and that there are no pins in the rubber, that the wheels are still far from getting thin and worn. She pats the side of the car reassuringly, saying, "See that? It's all alright. Nothing to worry about."

She has, then, a profound feeling of being seen. Not watched, exactly, but viewed, as if through a window dimly. When she turns her head over her shoulder to look, the sand storm is too thick to see anything but a faint glint on the horizon, and she makes towards it, letting go of the car and walking into the midst.

In the middle of the sand storm, there's a translucent ghost of buildings that once stood there, squat concrete housing units, high fences, no watchtower to speak of. A revenant flag of Arizona waves in the wind, showing the blood-stained star, an amiable Saguaro growing from a mound of crawling flesh. She doesn't need to recognize the specific compound to recognize the structure of the once-standing Gila River Internment Camp, having been torn to the ground long before. She imagines, if a ghost is made of the simmering anger and withering sadness after the human soul is long gone, than the same can happen to a building, and as she walks into the ghostly structure, she notices it idly moving, gliding aimlessly in the opposite direction of her, as though being dragged away by the winds, unmoored and unmourned. She sits down in the sand and watches it drift off, the walls and fences moving through her, unaffected, and she puts her head in her hands.

She loves the state of Arizona. There is no escaping the state of Arizona. The whole of it was built on blood and atrocities. It is beyond forgiving, to the very fine marrows.

There is another figure, sitting a distance away, vaguely human, with their head turned up to the star-studded sky, their mouth opens wide without a sound coming out of it. She wishes she'd taken Jacob Waltz with her, to tell her what kind of circle this is, what layer of hell. She turns her back to the figure, even as she sees them, from the corner of her eyes, get up and walk towards her. Instead, she looks again at the stars, which are as many as she's ever seen. She finds the three parts of Argo Navis, the ship of Odysseus, finds the hull, the deck, the sails, and looks at Canopus, the second-brightest star in the night sky. She thinks back. Tries to remember a time she was happy.

She knows the figure is right behind her by the breath on the nape of her neck, the feeling of damp warmth, the shape of an open mouth closing around the crown of her head, the flat ape teeth grinding down and gnawing wetly on her head, aiming to go down all the way to her skull. She doesn't hesitate to bring up her hand, slowly, and the gun she got from the

60

vending machine in it, and shoots the figure straight through their brain. It's a very loud sound. Her ears pop.

Sleeper Car only lets herself look at the body once afterwards. It's a withered, deprived figure, naked and rawboned, featureless as though sanded down with glasspaper. Their shot-through face is a red blooming flower, a poppy, a carnation. She finds her car again and vomits while leaning against the driver door. She coughs twice. Spits out a bullet casing.

They start driving again as soon as they can see the road.

* * *

The next morning, the car engine overheats, and they spend an hour or so cooling it off on the side of the road.

"There's your problem," Jacob Waltz says, when she pours water off on the engine and it steams like a skillet. "It's too fucking hot, that's the problem."

"I didn't notice," she says, dryly. She spends the next hour or so cooling the engine off to the best of her ability, pouring off coolant, checking the hoses, venting the car, sweet-talking the engine like a dog with heat exhaustion, until it relaxes, and she can get back inside.

She hasn't even had a chance to turn the car back on when a jogger shows up in the mirror, running their direction, right in the middle of the highway. He's a column of smoke in the rear-view mirror, billowing like a wildfire. When he approaches, he pauses only for a moment to lean down and look at her through her window, his face is all gone, or maybe he never had a face at all. His eyes are two black pinholes in a roaring pillar of red fire, waving like a flag.

"Heya," he says, super friendly. "Do you guys need a hand over there? Do you need me to call Triple A for you?"

"No, no thank you," she says. "We had a bit of a hiccup in our giddyup, but we're good to go now."

"Oh, good!" the jogger says, genuinely elated. "Don't be afraid to stop and ask for help, alright? You have a good one!" and then he merrily runs off, a single burning speck on the middle of the highway.

"Looks like we're in the circle of traitors after all," Jacob Waltz says, looking at where the jogger disappeared on the horizon. "Not that much longer to go."

* * *

The circle of traitors, or so Jacob Waltz says, is full of fucking bugs.

"Why are there so many fucking bugs?" Show Low says, once they've taken a break at the hottest hours of the day to nap, clean the car windshields from said many fucking bugs, and sip a pair of cold-ish ciders that Show Low managed to procure from somewhere, the way Show Low does. "What did bugs do? Bugs can't do treachery."

"What about when you think there's a bee in the house and you try to herd it out gently to make sure it's safe, but then it just turns out to be a strange-looking fly?" Sleeper says.

Jacob Waltz, ambling curiously across the hood of the car merrily in search of a live meal, says, "What about when you think a butterfly is a poisonous Monarch, but they're actually a nice tasty snack for you, but they're just mimicking the appearance of a Monarch to scare you off?"

"I don't really think either of those count as treachery," Show Low says, but just about then, the passenger comes back from where he was pissing in the bushes, and picks up his bottle of cider again, which Show Low had handed to him earlier, Sleeper Car not daring to acknowledge his presence even now, and he puts his full lips to the mouth of the bottle, bats his full lashes over his full monolid eyes, and she lets herself look at him, just for a prolonged moment, before he blows air over the bottle and it resonates beautifully.

Show Low laughs, and tries to do the same with hers, but her bottle is too full and it doesn't resonate right, just blows hollow, but that just makes her laugh harder. Looking at her, she asks, "Show Low, if there was a passenger in the car with us, do you think I'd know them?"

Her grin turns confused, and she says, "What are you asking me for?" but the passenger blows across his bottle again, a happy, affirmative note.

"Do you think, if there was a passenger in the car with us and I knew them, they'd be what I was going to the Underworld for?"

This time, Show Low doesn't try to respond, but she nods, playing along, when the passenger repeats the note again, in agreement.

"And, d'you reckon, Show Low, that if there was a passenger in the car with us and I knew them, and they'd be what I was going to the Underworld for, they'd be dead?"

This time, Show Low frowns at the exact same time the passenger intentionally flubs his breath of air over the neck of the bottle, creating the same hollow sound Show Low made earlier.

Show Low says, "I don't think it's a matter of alive or dead, exactly. It's katabasis. You go down to the Underworld because you wouldn't be able to live with yourself if you didn't try to. Because everyone deserves someone to go down to the Underworld for them."

It takes them another fifteen, twenty minutes, maybe half an hour, to finish cleaning up the car until it's decent enough to drive, and by that point, the ciders are done and she's just sitting up in the driver seat with the door propped open, waiting to sober up, when Jacob Waltz hisses sharply and ducks behind the steering wheel, tucking himself against the speedometer. It takes her yet another moment to see it, the blue and red of the tarantula hawk wasp crawling along the length of the car window, fluttering its wings.

It's a beautiful insect, which is a strange thing to think, but it is. Its body is a keen metallic glint, cobalt like carbon steel, its wings vibrant red like a flesh wound, and at first, she doesn't think about protecting Jacob Waltz at all when she puts her hand out to it, she just thinks that it's a beautiful thing, like a Wyoming quarter, and that she'd like to hold it. It crawls happily along into the fleshy pad of her thumb, and traces its limbs along her hand. The second thing she thinks about - still not defensive - is that tarantula hawk wasps rank pretty high on the Schmidt pain index. Short and electric was the way she'd heard it described. It would hurt tremendously, being stung by this creature.

Thirdly, she thought about Jacob Waltz, cowering behind the steering wheel, sitting up on his back legs with his pedipalps raised and hissing, and she doesn't even think again before crushing the tarantula hawk wasp in her hand.

It stings - of course it stings, and she adds a correction to the Schmidt scale: short, electric, and intimate.

Once, when Sleeper Car was 14, she rode her bike out on the street in the bike lane on the way to the Sprouts - this was in the summer and her mom was at work - and a bank truck ran her off the road and into a cemented-over ditch. She broke her arm in three places, and for a while she lay down on the hot cement, getting burned by God, the white bone jutting out of the top layer of skin, like new teeth breaking through the gumline. It hurt so much it didn't feel like anything at all.

There are 17,000 touch receptors and free nerves in the

human palm, and as she walks out of the car and goes down on her knees in the sand, she thinks every single one of them is the face of a person she met on the street who later went on to die a horrible death, unbeknownst to her.

It only lasts five minutes, and she counts every second in her head, but even after the five minutes, the pain only becomes a background noise. She doesn't think it'll ever go away completely. When she can feel her arms again, she's aware now that there are four hands caging her in place, that there's the hot muzzle of a pistol held up above her head, and that she clipped a hole in Show Low's side trying to shoot herself in the temple. On her other side, the passenger holds her gun hand in a trembling vice grip.

Show Low takes one hand off the back of her shoulder and uses her hand to tweak her ear. "It's only a bullet," she says, "I'm already gone."

* * *

"Have you ever been to Mexico?" Show Low asks from the backseat, afterwards.

"No," Sleeper Car says. She tried to, once, tried to cross over to Mexico, it wasn't a long drive, but everybody knows that the border is where the Furies are, with their Harris' hawk wings and their smiling, sharp-toothed faces who would eat the liver from your torso if they caught you trying to cross with doubt in your heart, and she was full of doubt, and lost her nerve before she even saw the first shadow of a hawk above her Hyundai.

"It's a beautiful place, Mexico," Show Low says. "You should go. You should go sometime."

"I want to apologize," she says, a little while after that.

"What for?" Show Low asks, having stuffed a bunch of

rolled-up napkins from the Chili's into the not-bleeding bullet hole in her side.

"Earlier," Sleeper Car says, "I said Four Peaks. I meant to say Four Corners. Four Peaks is the name of a brewery."

There is a long silence in the car, and then the passenger laughs. It's the sound of rushing water.

* * *

The Salt River is a live artery in the body of the desert, fresh and green, dotted with the brown bodies of wild horses standing in the stream, the gray-brown bodies of wild burros chewing weeds around the banks. They are quiet and content as they park up next to the lip of the river, four burros rolling their eyes at them, not spooked in the least. She takes out the last bullet in her gun, lays it on the flat of her tongue, and swallows it.

Show Low is the first out of the car, going down on one knee in front of the Salt River and cupping up a handful of water with both hands to drink. When Sleeper Car looks at her, her eyes skip over her, like a bobcat hidden in the brush, she just blends into the surroundings.

"Show Low," she says, and she looks up at her. Her face is relaxed.

"I think this is where I go," she says. "Yeah. Yeah, this feels like where I go. It's been a pleasure, Sleeper Car."

The water is green and muddy brown, and Sleeper Car sees a human hand floating down it, then a whole person, their eyes closed and their lips moving soundlessly under the surface of the water. The horses do not mind the floating bodies traveling downriver.

"It's been a pleasure, Show Low."

She gets into the water, then, all the way to her hips, and

then lays down, folds her hands on her chest, and lets the gentle current take her. "It's not so bad, you know," Show Low says, in the moments before she becomes just another body peacefully floating down the Salt River. "It's really not so bad at all."

And then she's gone.

"You know," Jacob Waltz says, perched on her shoulder. "This is where we part, too. From here I go up the mountains, to find my kind, to court and be eaten and be born again. It's been a fun ride, with you. I'm happy I went."

"I'm happy, too."

"Say, Sleeper. Have you ever been to Utah?"

Sleeper Car smiles. "I have once, not for very long. It's a beautiful place, Utah. Nowhere like it."

"Nowhere like it," he echoes. "Not too late to turn around, after all. You can still go back in your car. Drive home."

"Yeah," she says. Then she puts Jacob Waltz down and goes back to her car, sits down in the driver's seat. Turns the engine on, and then off again.

"Forgot my keys," she says, when she comes back. "Didn't want to be locked out, you know."

"Fuck you," Jacob Waltz says, laughing. "You're such a fucking asshole."

"Best of luck to you, Jacob Waltz. I hope you find what you're looking for."

"Best of luck to you, Sleeper Car. I hope you find what you're looking for."

She gets into the water while looking backwards at the car, and at the tarantula on the shoreline, letting herself fall into the current back-first. It seems a lot faster and a lot more violent when it carries her away.

* * *

She wakes up around a campfire she doesn't remember lighting, sitting in front of an old mineshaft entry that goes steeply down into the Godless abyss. It's night. There are three coyotes sitting on the other side of the fire. When she looks around, she's otherwise alone, but a hand closes around her own, even if she can't see the person it belongs to.

"Welcome to the lowest ring of Hell," one coyote says. "You've made it pretty far down. Only down the mineshaft to go, you know, and there you will meet the King of the Mine."

"Who are you?" she asks.

The second coyote says, "I am To Amble."

The third says, "I am To Pace."

The first says, "I am To Lope. We are the Hounds of Hell."

"I didn't think that was the traditional narrative purpose of coyotes. Seems out of place if you don't mind me saying."

To Amble licks its paws, and grins at her, cackling. "What do you know about the traditional narrative purpose of coyotes? You don't know the real name of any landmark you've crossed on the way here."

She turns her head down, abashed. To Lope looks to agree, but nips at To Amble's ear. "You expected Hell to have hounds, and so, here we are. It's not our usual purpose, but we go where we are needed."

To Pace inches towards her on the fire. "There is a penance, you know. To go down to the hall of the King, you must pay a toll. We are hungry. Give me your right hand."

Sleeper Car thinks on that. "I need it to drive back to Phoenix," she says, "to change gears while I grip the steering wheel."

To Pace considers this, and asks again. "Give me your right foot, then."

Again, she says, "I need it to drive back home, in order to press on the gas pedal."

68

Finally, he growls, and asks, "Give me your right eye, then." and she can't think of an answer to that, so she lets To Pace circle around the campfire and come all the way to her face, and he pulls the eye from her skull and swallows it in one gulp, then returns to sit amongst its siblings.

Then, To Amble says, "I am hungry also. Give me your right atrium, so I may eat it."

She thinks about it, and says, "No, that would kill me, and I need it to keep going into the mineshaft."

To Amble asks again, "Then give me your right lung, and I'll eat that."

With COVID still as prevalent as it is, she could use every lung she has. "No, I need that too, or I may collapse on the way back."

Finally, To Amble yawns impatiently and says, "Then give me your right kidney." And she can't think of a way to contradict that fast enough, so To Amble also crosses around the campfire and walks behind her, to pull the red kidney from her back, taking it in its mouth and rejoining its siblings, happily gnawing on it.

Third and last, To Lope looks at her, looks through her straight to the other side. "I am also hungry," To Lope says. "Give me your right mind, so I may eat it."

She says, "I'll need my right mind in order to make it down the mineshaft to meet the King. Take something else."

"Fine," To Lope says. "Give me your right way, then."

"I'll need my right way to make it home again at the end of my journey," she says. "I can't give that to you."

Finally, To Lope snarls, and brings its face to the light of the fire, showing the unhinged yellow eyes of a wild animal. "Then give your right place," she says, and Sleeper Car can't think of a response to that, so To Lope walks across the fire, through the flame, and eats the right place from her hands, leaving her feeling unmoored and unsteady, listing like a dead leaf.

"There," To Lope says. "Now, you are dead to rights. You may go down the mineshaft to meet the King of Hell."

The entry to the mine is a highway exit in the dark, only visible in loose shapes, the curve of their feet bends towards it and the urge to go where they are called. She hopes it's their exit, and ducks her head down as she enters, even though it's big enough to fit her. Every step she takes, another echoes behind her, and when she reaches her hand back, someone's familiar hand wraps around hers. It's the hand she's seen chew fingernails, screw together IKEA furniture, hold tight to a phone to take smiling selfies, it is the passenger's hand, who walks every step behind her.

The passenger, unseen, holds her hand all the way down. Without the light of God to shine their way, their only source of guidance is the occasional gas lamp, flickering above, though there is a definite feeling that they could not possibly be alone here.

In the crevices of the mineshaft, eyes glint back, wet and red with mine dust, and though she can see no miner in the flesh, sometimes a gas lamp swings, revealing the playing silhouettes of workers decanting the earth in search of conductive metals, like shadow puppets. From down, down below, she can hear the squeaking of wheels, and keeps walking down the mineshaft. It is too big for one person, and too small for two, so she and the passenger keep hovering between walking side-by-side and walking one behind the other, finding themselves knocking shoulders and trembling like insects crawling up a car windshield.

It goes for a long, long time, then. The mineshaft gets hotter and more damp, like the wet gut of the earth unspooling to reveal miles of long intestine.

Near the very end of it, it stops looking like a mineshaft, and starts to look ancient and unrefined, the mouth of a burial cave cut with stone pickaxe. The flooring is too uneven for wheelbarrows, and when Sleeper Car's foot knocks against an unpolished stone jutting out, the passenger behind her has to reach out to grab her arm. She says, unthinkingly, "Argo, Argo."

She cannot see him in the dark of the cave, but she hears the sound of a burbling creek, a pot of water set to boil and just starting to murmur to itself. You don't know the smell of fresh water until you've been deprived of it for a long time.

The end of the mineshaft curls into a poorly lit dome, and there's a man at the center, pushed against the wall. He's sitting on a little stool, polishing his glasses with the oiled fabric of his mining shirt. He has a short beard, which is thick black with soot and appears tacky to the touch from sweat. To the side of him, he has a modest wooden cart full of copper ingots, completely in the raw and nowhere near done putrefying for casting into coins or shaping into computer wires. From the thigh down, his legs are that of a bighorn sheep, covered in coast beige fur and ending in short, mean-looking hooves. He looks busy, his face lined with wrinkles like an old denim shirt, but otherwise an amiable sort of man, with a friendly expression between his pinched eyebrows.

"Hm," he says, not unfriendly. "Can I help you?"

"Are you the King of the Hell?" she asks.

"I am," he says, humbly. "I am the plutocrat of precious metal, the Union Organizer of all copper miners, the barrowman of burrows, the Hewer of the Underworld. I'm the Brakesman of the winding engine, and I decide where each soul goes. What do you trouble me for? I have only a brief minute for lunch, and then I must get back to work. There are mines to be dug, there are miners to break, so speak quick."

Not mincing any words, Sleeper Car says, "I am here to

find someone who does not belong in your employ, and bring him back with me."

"What is his name?" the King of Hell asks, and starts to palm about in his oily shirt, fishing out a fountain pen and a little checkered notebook, as though used to account for shifts taken and yet to be taken. He sets his glasses back on his face, none the cleaner for his careful treatment of them just before. He squints at his journal, then looks at her with an odd, sympathetic frown. "What is his name?" he asks.

"His name is The Argonaut."

Again, the King of the Underworld looks, running his pen up and down the page methodically before clicking his tongue with displeasure. "I'm stumped," he says, "The Argonaut is nowhere on here."

"He is not anywhere on your list," she says, "because he is not dead."

The King of the Underworld looks at her, despondent, like he gets that kind of answer all the time. "Yes, I know," he says, "the lower circles are for the living, after all, girl, and the dead are much harder to put to work. The dead, you know, demand lunch breaks, even smoke breaks, and pay raises, and to be treated like human beings. The living makes no such demands of me."

"Is he dead?"

"It doesn't matter what he is, he's mine."

The King of Hell laughs, and she imagines he must like that answer. "Well, alright," he says. "Well, alright. If you can lead him out, you can take him with you, if he's yours to begin with, I won't stop you. But there's a fee, you know - if you want something of your own, you must give me something of mine, and I will only give you the one chance." And he puts out one dirty, smudged hand, one soot-covered hand, one wrinkled old handkerchief of a hand.

She doesn't have to think about it. She takes the Wyoming quarter out of her pocket and deposits it in the King of Hell's palm. He looks at it suspiciously. "This isn't made in Arizona," he says.

"No," she says. "But it came from the earth, and it is beautiful. It's a treasure, and it is yours, plutocrat."

With that, he smiles once more, and puts the coin in his cart, with all of his copper ingots. "I should get back to work," he says, something like fondness in his voice. "Don't let my dogs catch you on the way out."

They walk out of the mineshaft, hands clasped together. They walk out of the river. They walk out of the shore and back into the four-seater car, and they both collapse into their respective seats with a sigh. "God," The Argonaut groans. "God, that was exhausting. Do you think we can stop in a hotel or something on the way back?"

"No, fuck that," Sleeper Car says. "It's only, what? Three hours? Let's just go home."

So, they do.

THE RAIN DRUM

BY ANTHONY MARTELLO

Reyan works with his parents at the *Blue Spirit Coffee Plantation* that lays nestled along the foothills of a Sri Lankan jungle. Because of his vitiligo, his parents have him work indoors packing up treated coffee beans into big canvas bags for shipping and delivery. Every day he dreams about dancing in the sunshine and playing with the other kids in the jungle. One afternoon he hears laughter and giggles in the distance, so he steps outside, peering into the exciting unknown. As he walks out onto the warehouse deck, big streaks of white illuminate across his face and arms. "Reyan, return to the warehouse, I don't want you to burn again. Remember your face and arms were as red as Kashmiri pepper, and remember how much you cried?"

"Yes mother." I hear some kids playing in the crops, they might be stealing beans again."

Whether there were kids or not, Rayan found that he often had to lie. At age six, the village children would tease him, calling him, "white leopard." His white patches clashed against his tan Sri Lankan skin. To avoid the teasing, he instead spent long days counting the beans, sorting them, and packing them for the customers. Working in the dusty haze, he skims the blue beans from the top of the crop and hoards them like precious gems. When he returns home in the afternoon, he stores them in his orange-red kalaya jug decorated with tall palm trees and exotic floral designs.

One day while Reyan's parents are picking ripe cherries on the terraces, he wanders into the outskirts of the plantation and the jungle. *I'll just stay below the canopy in the shade, that way I won't burn.* He shuffles across the slope down into the dense jungle floor by the creek flowing through the ravine. The water appears lower and the creek bank drier than last months when his dad took him hiking down to the creek. His father takes him every few months to check the water level and make sure there is enough supply to irrigate the coffee farm. This time, Reyan wades across the creek that flows knee-high and ventures further into the dense part of the jungle. Natural light breaks through the green cracks in the canopy roof, radiating humid light onto his vividly white skin where the white streaks and patches warm with life.

He grows thirsty and sweat drips from his wiry white hair. He encounters a pitcher plant and lifts the lid off the green plant in search of water when suddenly, it bites down on his finger, "Ouch, my, my finger..." Reyan jumps.

The surprisingly voracious plant lets go, "Well, what do you expect? I am a carnivore. I couldn't resist a finger-tip appetizer before a Grizzled squirrel supper."

"Wha, what? You can't eat a squirrel; you don't have teeth."

"Yes, but I have a belly the size of a water jug and a thirst-quenching appeal, wouldn't you say?" The strange plant's lid lifts up and down when it speaks. He is more mysterious than he is dangerous when he speaks.

"You sure do," Reyan replies.

"I just collect fresh droplets of water from the canopy on my lid and wait for the squirrels to get thirsty and come scurry in for a drink... and then, wham! I capture them and enjoy a Grizzled squirrel dinner."

"Where can I find water?" asks Reyan.

"Down at the creek, but hurry because it is slowly drying up," warns the mystical plant.

"Okay, I will hurry. Thank you for your help."

"My pleasure. Come and visit me any time. I may be rooted in the ground, but have many large friends...the smaller ones, of course, are afraid of me but I chat often with the larger of the species."

Reyan discovers a pool along the banks of the creek and reaches down to drink. He cups his hands and drinks. He reaches out for more and sees the reflection of a monkey jumping from tree to tree. It belts out a sharp screech a few times and then hangs from its tail on the branch of a tree close to the water's surface. A purple reflection reverberates off the monkey's face. He has a branch of yellow and red coffee cherries in his hand and he peels off of the beans and spits them out into the creek.

The monkey screeches once briefly and then faces Reyan. "You ought to try these, the peels are delightful and fruity, and so invigorating."

Reyan, appalled, cries out, "no, you must not. My father will trap you and relocate you across the island. We can't have monkeys eating our crops."

The monkey replies addictively, "but I can't help myself, I can't stop eating them, and I can jump higher than the other monkeys and climb faster than a squirrel can jump!"

"Well, I am warning you, purple monkey, that my daddy will catch you and send you far away."

The monkey swings away and Reyan returns to the plantation. What a wonderful day for Reyan; he discovers two new friends living there right below his coffee farm. He knows he must return to his sheltered life of hiding from the sun but can't wait to revisit his friends.

That night, Reyan sits on the couch reading *National Geographic* that was given to him by a traveling geologist studying minerals in the foothills surrounding the farm. He spent some time tasting the coffee and beans and would tell Reyan stories about his adventures. He told Reyan that endless treasures can be found in the rainforest and that all you have to do is search with curiosity and wonder. As Reyan escapes into his magazine, his parents discuss their day at work with a higher tone than usual. Reyan's father, concerned, asks, "Jyoti, did you notice, today, how the irrigation canals were drier?"

She replies, "We haven't had as much rain for the last two months, I think it will eventually come back. Krish, why don't you record the water depth for the next thirty days and I will talk with the others about their observations."

Originally planted and developed by Reyan's great-grandfather, The Blue Spirit Coffee farm employs five different families in the south-western region of Sri Lanka. Each family depends on the crops to produce high-quality beans for sale locally, and throughout the mainland of India. Because of the water shortage concerns, Jyoti and Krishi decide to host a business board meeting on the premises to discuss measuring the water flow into the farm and how to address any questions.

They congregate and discuss, "Thank you for coming to discuss our concerns about irrigation and the rainfall. Let us know if you have any ideas on how to address the shortfall of water for the last two months."

Reyan, once again, hears the concern from the adults in his life about the lack of precious water for the farm. *The next time I see the Pitcher Plant, I will tell him we need water.* And, of course, it is another reason to venture off into the forbidden jungle and visit his friends.

The next day after the meeting, while his parents are on the higher slope, tending to the cherries and measuring water flow, Reyan travels further into the jungle. He walks a mile more than yesterday, deeper into the dense trees and latticed vines that crawl to the top of the canopy like a giant green spider web connecting all the creatures. On the branch of a montane tree rests a chameleon with a red-purple hue that contrasts the green-yellow leaves of the tree. The red left eye of the chameleon independently rotates from the purple right eye, keeping the focus on Reyan as he approaches the brilliant reptile.

"Machan, what happened to your skin?"

Reyan replied, "Oh, hello rainbow lizard. I have vitiligo."

"It looks like *god* struck you with lightning, machan" the chameleon chuckles.

"My mother told me *Vishnu* appeared and kissed me when I was born."

"Hmm, interesting, you must have an important mission for people."

"None of the village kids want to play with me, they call me white leopard."

"They are just jealous because they were not kissed by a god." The chameleon continues... "My name is Kami, and I am a Panther chameleon."

Reyan giggles, "Can I call you rainbow lizard?"

"Sure, machan, but I want to be green."

"But you have such bright colors. I have streaks of white, but you shine so brightly!" Reyan proclaims.

Song by Kami:

78

While you might find delight
in my rainbow bright sight,
let me share with you my plight.

I want to be green
Who wants to be seen?
Please hide me from this scene
I want to be green.

When the girls shuffle by
I lose my disguise
I will never compromise...
I want to be green.

Kami's tail curls up into a fiddle and he plays it like a violin.

I may appear purple and red
But it won't go to my head
I want to be green and out of sight
An ordinary garden green delight

I want to be green.

Rayan laughs, enjoys Kami's song and comments, "But, I would love to have brilliant colors like you and entertain all the kids in the village."

Kami quiets down and replies, "I become very embarrassed and shy; I just want to blend in." While Kami is sharing his innermost fears, Amber, a pink female chameleon, shuffles down from around the other side of the tree. Kami blushes into bright purples and reds. "See, machan, my skin is on fire, and I can't control my embarrassment."

Amber winks at Kami. He becomes even more self-conscious. "I just want to be green like the other garden variety lizards. I have a hard time blending in."

"Blending in is something you should do naturally, Kami. Oh, Kami, oh, my poor Kami," a voice interrupts from the bushes.

"Cassie, is that you? What are you doing here? You didn't see that, did you?" Kami pleads toward the voice in the bushes.

Reyan sees the creature in the bushes, "Hey, Kami look at those yellow eyes."

"That is Cassie, the golden palm civet cat!" exclaims Kami. "She loves to sneak up on people."

"That's right. Sneaking is the only way to hypnotize intruders with my glare." Cassie enlightens Reyan. She jumps out of the bush. Her eyes blare with golden light from the day. She smiles and chuckles at Kami, "I saw you freeze up like a purple popsicle when Amber shuffled by you. I think she likes you!" Kami continues, "Why are you so afraid of her?"

Kami answers, "She always surprises me, and I lose control of my chromatophores, and I blush in rainbow attire, and any garden variety chameleon should be able to just blend into green and yellow, but not me."

Cassie reassures him, "You are lucky, you guys are the only species I know that can trans-flash into brilliant colors...I wish I could, it would help me on my midnight missions."

Kami raises a suspicious eyebrow toward Cassie, "What midnight missions are you referring to?"

Cassie exclaims, "Blue Spirit Coffee cherry raids! There's a village in India buying our poop for 5700 Rupee per bag."

Kami laughs as green and gold flashes briefly through his

reptilian skin. Reyan jumps in, "I don't believe you; my parent's coffee only sells for 1500 Rupee per bag."

Cassie replies, "I am as serious as the white streaks on your skin, machan. Yep, as long as I keep eating red and yellow coffee cherries, I can produce a premium product. Ching, ching," Dollar signs appear in Cassie's eyes. "We eat the whole cherry, peel and all, then the next day, walla! Golden Palm Civet Cat poop at your service. We are the golden geese of the rainforest."

Reyan cracks up. "You can come work with us, pooping out civet coffee, so you don't have to steal it."

The opportunistic Cassie agrees and dances toward Reyan in song.

As you sit and you gaze
All you may see is a cat
With bright eyes

Lazy at times
I'll sleep in a tree
But don't be fooled
Beneath my disguise
Is a golden surprise

I'm greater than gold...
And so, I've been told
I have them all sold

I'm greater than gold...

And, as you sit and gaze-keep gazing, please do.
I produce this savory bean
I'm greater than gold...

You know me as Cassie
But when I do my trade
Let it be known,
They call me Cashie.

I'm greater than gold
Let it be told,
They call me Cashie

The tradesmen they come
The tradesmen they go
They call me Cashie

Dollar signs show in her eyes and cash registers sound off, "ching, ching"

They package my poop
Scoop after scoop
They call me Cashie

I'll send it away
As far as Bombay
They call me Cashie

Reyan, inspired, proclaims, "I want you to come with me and meet my parents. They could make so much more money and you could help all the people in our village." Reyan walks back toward the plantation and Cassie and Kami slowly follow him. They approach the Pitcher Plant that Reyan met on his first adventure the previous day.

A loud belch emanates from his lid. "Yummy, that was a delicious snack. I just finished off a turquoise tarantula. It had a brilliant coat of green on its exoskeleton, brilliant creature, but I need fiber too..."

Kami yells, "You are an abomination to the rainforest. I will make sure I get nowhere near your snap trap, Pitcher Plant."

"Ha, ha," the plant laughed horribly. "I am here to keep you consumers in check, and besides, I watch everything-look out behind you kids-here comes a purple-faced monkey playing catch with a bright blue rock."

They all turn around as the monkey stops in a tree above. He tantalizes them by playing catch with himself, throwing this mysterious blue rock up in the air, catching it and hanging it below for the crowd to see. Brilliant rays of blue light emanate from the chunk of raw rock in his hands.

The Pitcher Plant's lid starts moving, "What do we have here, purple monkey?"

"Hee, hee, haw, haw. I found this in the valley above the slithering stream where all those machines are shooting water into the side of the mountain."

"Oh, I see, you are bored with the rainforest variety of husks, fronds, and vines," the wise plant continues.

Reyan interjects, "May I see that rock?"

"No way, white machan. This is my jungle treasure."

"Will you let me hold it for a minute if I give you these?" Reyan pulls out a handful of yellow coffee cherries and offers them to the monkey. The monkey grabs a cherry and sniffs. A delightful smile fills the monkey's face.

"Hmm, okay, but give it back after one minute."

The monkey hands Reyan the rock.

Kami notices, "Oh my greatness, Machan, your white patches have turned a radiant blue. Amazing!"

Cassie confidently educates, "What you are holding is a sapphire rock, Machan, and you could buy a thousand bags of coffee with that one chunk of beautiful mineral."

Mr. Pitcher (plant) advises, "Reyan, you must go and find

the source and tell your father so he can sell them and make money for the plantation and villagers." *Reyan knows he must keep his new friends and discovers a secret.*

The monkey chews the yellow coffee cherry carps and spits out the seeds. Cassie screams, "No, save those."

Reyan gives the sapphire rock back to the monkey and picks up the partially digested beans and hands them to Cassie. "Thank you, partner. I will add these to my cash-stash."

Reyan digs deeper into his pocket and pulls out five more red coffee cherries this time. "Monkey, I will trade you these five red coffee cherries for your blue rock. The red ones are sweeter than the yellows."

Salivating from delightful addiction, the monkey glances at the rock and then looks back at the red cherries. His eyes bounce back and forth for a few seconds and then he agrees, "Ok, I'll enjoy these with my friends." He hands over the blue sapphire and swings away into the rainforest.

Then, as if struck by lightning a second time in his young life, Reyan springs into action. "Kami, I know you want to be green, but I have a job for you. I need you to be as wonderful as your rainbow colors can be but blend into blue. Go investigate with Cassie where these rocks are and what those machines are doing, but don't be seen. Let me know what you find..."

Cassie adds, "Kami, you can ride on my back, and I will evaluate the scene for blue rocks and their value."

"Okay my friends, I have to go back home but let's meet here by Mr. Pitcher tomorrow at this time." Reyan returns home.

Meanwhile, Kami's chromatophores dial into a yellow gold that matches Cassie's fur. He jumps on her back as they prance their way through the valley floor up onto the higher plateau above the slithering stream. The stream curves like a huge green snake in the rainforest. They follow the bends and banks upstream. When they get tired, they stop to drink from the creek. Cassie laps up some water as Kami scans the right side of the embankment with his right eye and then independently and simultaneously scans the left side of the forest with his left eye where he spots a white leopard stalking them with its engaging eyes. Kami whispers without moving a bit, "Cassie, don't look behind you but please realize there is a huge, white cat much more ferocious than you, locking beams on us right now."

Cassie returns an ensuring whisper to Kami, "Okay, I know you chameleons are masters at freezing and blending in so, all I can say is hang on tight, and when the white beast springs forward, squeeze me with your catcher's mitt claws. A few seconds later the jungle predator jumps out of the green and directly toward them. Kami obliges and pinches Cassie, signaling her. She reacts instantly and pulls a backflip from the creek bank onto a Montane tree branch hanging over the water. It is the most invigorating ride Kami has ever experienced. He holds on tightly to her fur with his bi-clasps and moves quicker than any chameleon in reptilian existence. Cassie climbs up to the top of the tree escalating them higher. The predator follows up the base of the trunk and gazes at them. Cassie jumps even higher at the top where the branches are smaller, and no large cat could reach. They wait as the white leopard tires. Then he finally strolls back into the dense jungle.

When Reyan returns home, he digs his hands into the kalaya jug with the choice blue coffee beans. He takes the sapphire rock out of his pocket, wipes the dirt off of it, and compares it to his grey-blue coffee beans. He opens his coveted National Geographic magazine and discovers refined and cut blue sapphires as a final product in an article about refining raw gemstones. He is awe struck at the radiance of color compared to his savory coffee beans. *One captures the eye and captivates us all with brilliance, while the other stimulates taste buds for grown-ups to enjoy and chat time away.* Even though he enjoys the taste of coffee and milk, the blue sapphires become more interesting to him suddenly. He may truly be hypnotized by Cassie and her song, after all!

At the dinner table, he asks his mom, "Mother, how much are blue sapphires worth?"

Jyoti smiled with curiosity, "Oh, let me see, for the large bright blue pure, natural sapphires, they are worth about 10 bags of our premium *Mountain Blue Blend* (1500 Rupee) so that would be about 3500 Rupee.

"What made you think of that, Reyan?" Jyoti dug further.

"I read about them in my *National Geographic Magazine.*" he carefully replies.

"Did you know that the largest blue sapphire ever found was right here in Sri Lanka?" Jyoti educates Reyan.

"No, I want to find some. Can I go some time, Mother?"

Jyoti's face muscles tighten as she replied, "No, my machan, it is too dangerous in the forest, there are mines where the sapphires are found."

Reyan tests her further, "But, mother, I want to see what the blue rocks look like and I want to collect some big sapphires."

"No, machan. Get back to your homework."

Reyan waits for his mother to leave the room. He then decides to dive into another story and picks up his magazine where he left off last time. In the other room, he hears his mother and father discussing the water supply levels and their weeks' observation on the terraces.

"Jyoti, something is very wrong. Our readings are half of the previous three months of water supply."

Worried, she asks, "what will we tell the board?"

Krishi is silent, then responds. "I don't know yet. we may

have to take out a loan and buy water from another province, our bean count has reduced by 20% and our quality appears to have suffered."

Jyoti adds, "During our tasting yesterday, I felt like the beans were a little too acidic."

That night Reyan falls asleep worried but full child-like anticipation for tomorrow and the wonders of the jungle.

When Cassie and Kami cargo finally reach the higher stream, they approach the edge of the forest and come upon the loud water jets blasting streams of water into the mountainside. Above the commotion, closer to the headwaters is a huge pool of water resting beneath a man-made dam where they water for the hydraulic jets that blast the rock and soil open. The huge cemented dam reaches across the river and has created a giant wedge in the side of the mountain near the river. Cassie and Kami make sure to stay hidden in the canopy as they watch the disturbing operation of heavy machinery, jets, and destruction of the mother earth. Below the jets are narrow slurries where brilliant speckles of blue can be seen collecting in the sluice boxes at the bottom of the containers.

Cassie's eyes lock on a sight to behold. Kami can see the reflection in her eyes of a blue radiance she could only dream of. "Earth to Cassie, hey, hey, hey, wake up, Cashie!"

"Is that all you think about, money?"

"No, it's just so beautiful." The cash cat replies.

"Remember, we are here on a mission to help Reyan." Kami says.

"Okay, Kami, I know what to do. You see those baskets full of sapphire rocks, go down there and transform into a beautiful blue that matches those stones and wait until they carry them into the warehouse near the office of the mine."

Kami hesitates, "I don't know if I can do that. I am just a

little soft jungle lizard compared to those big machines, rocks, and dirty people."

Cassie encourages, "Come on Kami, this is probably one of the only times blending in is life-changing and life-saving for the forest and oh, and, not to mention when you are searching for a mate." Cassie laughs sarcastically. "If you get enough practice here, you may get it right with Amber the next time she drops in on your tree! Ha, ha."

"Why are you always spying on me? Can't I do anything in peace and solitude?"

"No, Kami, I am a curious cat and I watch everything, and besides, you are the most entertaining reptile in the rainforest."

Cassie continues, "Okay great Panther Chameleon, this is your chance, go ahead. I will wait here and chew on these palm kernels while you save the forest with your undercover chromatophores."

Kami laughs, "You will be waiting for a while. I have to shuffle over there to those containers."

She scratches her ear with her claw, "Okay, we will wait until the workers are working at the water and then we will dart across and I will drop you off on the crate."

Kami agrees, "Sounds quicker to me. Let's do it."

They wait for a short while and then see a clearing. Cassie jumps out into the opening, across the dirt and rocks, and drops Kami off into the blue container. He quickly blends into the blue. Cassie runs across the other side of the forest and waits in the dense green jungle. One can barely see her golden eyes ablaze with curiosity as Kami works his color magic. He waits and waits, and then a miner picks up the crate full of raw rocks and carries it into the warehouse. The worker puts the crate down. Kami hears a few men talking business about the mines and the dam blocking the water flow from the mountains.

"Mr. Raji, how do you plan on operating the new bottled water business?"

The two men in business suits with briefcases are interviewing Mr. Raji, a short, balding man with big black shiny eyes. He is wearing a maroon cashmere button-up shirt exotically decorated with palm trees and snake charmers, "Great question, you see that pool up there above the water blasters, I will utilize its source to bottle it up and sell it. It's a double cash cow."

One man takes his glasses off and gazes out at the operation in awe. The other man raises his eyebrows in intense curiosity. Mr. Raji slides over to the blue crate where Kami elegantly blends in. "I will give you guys 10% of my return and I will throw in five-carat blue sapphires for your wives."

The businessmen look closer. Mr. Raji grabs the rock right next to Kami's right mitt. He washes one-off under the sink water and dries it with a towel. "Take a look, just like a clear Sri Lankan sky with a touch of a cloud to accentuate the deep blue."

"Why the clouds?" asks one of the men.

Mr. Raji eagerly replies, "So you know they are not fake, they are not lab created like 90% the junk out there."

While the businessmen plot their double profit scheme, Cassie peeks around the corner of the warehouse door from the outside. Kami's right eye rotates and focuses on Cassie, near the door. Cassie waits patiently for the men to leave the room. When they finally leave, she prances into the warehouse, jumps up on the table with the blue container and grabs Kami. Kami clamps on and fades into gold again as they break away-out through the door and into the forest.

The next day while his parents read the water levels, Reyan joins Kami, and Cassie at the base of *Mr. Pitcher and his green lattice of roots that covertly integrate beneath the rainforest canopy.* "Hello Mr. Pitcher and investigators, what did you guys discover yesterday?"

Cassie drools and hisses with a funny smile, "We have a new undercover reptile *Houdini* that can appear and reappear as he pleases, and his name is Kami Leon of Sri Lanka!"

"Ha, ha," Cassie giggles.

Kami nods slowly and acknowledges Cassie's admiration. "But before we get to the juicy details, let me tell you about our jungle gymnastics performance to escape a hungry white leopard."

Kami jumps in, "It was the most exhilarating ride I have ever been on. A white leopard peeks his head out from the foliage and tries to attack us, then Cassie prompts me to hang on, so I clamp my mitts on her, and she does a backflip up into a tree and lands it!"

Cassie smiles and more drool drains out of the side of her mouth. "She then climbs to the top branches where the white beast could not reach us. I have never moved so fast. I was so alive!"

Reyan interrupts, "What a fun ride, but do you guys think I look a white leopard?"

Cassie replies, "No."

And Kami doubles that, "No" and Mr. Pitcher wisely shares, "You, my boy, look like a ray of scattered light that Shiva himself has bestowed upon you!"

Reyan perks up; his smiles brighten.

Then Cassie shares, "When we got to the water blasting machines, we found a sapphire mine with a huge wedge dug out of the side of the mountain and a cemented dam above the pool of water where they were blasting into the mines."

"Hmm, dams are forbidden in the rainforest. How are we to survive if someone is hoarding precious water from the heavens?" The Pitcher plant protests.

Kami jumps off Cassie's back onto a higher branch at eye level with Mr. Pitcher and spills the rotten coffee bean, "Mr. Raji, the owner of the sapphire mine has built a cement dam above his estate and is collecting water to divert to his hydraulic blasters. But it gets worse, he is planning on starting a bottled water company, utilizing the water from the dam."

Cassie, Kami's new sidekick chimes in, "He's double dipping in our forest. We must stop him!"

Reyan asks Mr. Pitcher, "Is that why the creeks have been low? My parents have been meeting with the board about it for the last two months."

Mr. Pitcher turns his oval head up and toward Reyan and Kami, "Yes, machan. We have found the water thief."

"Great job, my friends, the *shola* has spoken, and you have listened. Now that we know where the water is, we must devise a plan." Mr. Pitcher continues to inquire from his lid, "But, before we create a plan, I must ask, how did you learn of this information?"

Cassie, inspired by her sidekick, tells the story of how Kami transformed into blue to match the sapphires in the container and spy on the businessmen plotting their profits. Cassie replies to Mr. Pitcher and the gang, "For the first time Kami controlled his color and blended perfectly to his environment. First with my golden fur, then with the sapphires."

Mr. Pitcher proclaims, "Kami, I am most impressed with your adaptation and blending into your environment."

Kami blushes a bit into red and yellows, "Thank you, I think I might be getting the hang of color blending." Just as his confidence is building, Amber, a pink chameleon, shuffles by.

Kami, ablaze in his new identity, decides to show off and start doing push-ups in front of Amber. He toe-taps to the beat of the *rain drum*, enjoying the thunderous vibrations. He prances up and down, trying to impress Amber. When she slithers by, he winks at her slyly with his left eye, simultaneously using his right eye to lasso a locust with his sticky bubble gum tongue and then crunch it down noisily for her to hear.

Amber plays into his ego by alternately blinking her left and right eyelids, cooing circularly. She also churns out a little pinker on her back to pump him up. Kami's ego inflates even more. He captures a honey locust, dips it in another pitcher plant to sweeten it and rolls it up in his sticky tail. He then unravels his fiddlehead tail like a green carpet right in front of Amber. She lunges to capture the sticky locust, but Kami quickly curls it back up with his tail again.

"Ha, ha," she laughs sarcastically. *'Hmmm, she wonders, what can I do to get him back?'* Amber picks a ripe avocado with her tail and mashes it up with her mitts, then slides downstream of his branch, greasing up his perch. She then slithers below his branch and continues to blush in bright pink and yellow hues. Finding this irresistible, he stands up on his branch and heads down toward her when suddenly he slips out of control and lands in a puddle of water on the ground near his friends. Kami's friends laugh and she laughs hysterically. He slowly crawls out of the puddle, illuminating a bright blue color.

She retaliates, "You are the bluest Panther I have ever seen! Ha, ha," and crawls away into the misty jungle.

Cassie laughs hysterically, "It looks like blue is your color."

Reyan agrees, "I like you better in blue, too. Forget green, rainbow lizard, you are *Kami Leon,* the great blue Panther."

"Okay, humans and animals, let's get back to saving the forest and the Blue Spirit Coffee farm. If we don't stop Mr. Raji now, it will only get worse before we all dry up. Something your non-botanical types might not realize is that we trees and plants are all connected underground."

Reyan jumps in and asks Mr. Pitcher, "Let me guess, your roots can talk to each other?"

"Well, yeah, sort of machan, the sound is part of it."

Cassie, plays with Mr. Pitcher, "Now, you're going to give us some guru glob, glob about energy or vibrations, right?"

"Precisely," the wise carnivorous plant jokes, "We all have roots that sense vibrations and follow or dance to the source. Hence, we must convince every plant, shrub, and tree from here to Mr. Raji's mine to dance beneath the canopy."

Reyan adds, "Or how about an underground shuffle?"

The gang laughs.

"Yes, machan." Mr. Pitcher assures. "Tomorrow, let's meet here at noon to awaken the green lattice and roots that lie beneath the dam and sapphire mine."

Everyone returns home to get a good night's sleep. While Reyan is reading his *National Geographic Magazine*, he comes across pictures of kids playing the drums in Africa. He remembers that he was taking traditional Sri Lankan drum lessons earlier in the year. *Tomorrow I will bring my drum and entice the trees to dance with me to the dam.*

"START HERE" Reyan wants to share his secret with the kids in the village and even his parents but knows if he tells anyone, especially his parents, they would never leave him out of their sight. But today, when his parents leave to do their water readings, Reyan returns to the meeting spot (Pitcher plant's station) with his musical drum. "Machan, what do we have here?" the plant asked. "I brought the traditional Sri Lankan drum that I take lessons on." "Excellent, Light-boy. You brought sound and light today." Cassie arrives, chewing on yellow coffee beans. "Where is Kami?" "I don't know," Cassie pauses...

Reyan looks closer and sees a cone shaped eye moving in circles on Cassie's back. "Ha, ha, I got you, "Kami screams out loud. "Wow, you blended in perfectly, I didn't even see you," Reyan says. Mr. Pitcher clears his throat, "Gather around my friends, it is time to dance your way to the dam! We each will invite plants-big and small to do the lateral lunge, roots and all toward the dam. Like I said yesterday, roots grow toward vibrations and can expand in any direction." Mr. Pitcher continues to coach the crew: "Kami, since you're the slowest and smallest, you encourage the smaller plants around here." "Ok, Mr. Pitcher." Kami agrees. Second, Cassie participates, "I'll invite the medium-size plants and smaller trees." "And, Reyan," Mr. Pitcher continues, "I have a special assignment for you. I would like you to invite *Sharma*, one of the tallest trees near the dam, to dance with you. She was blessed by *Lakshmi*, goddess of good fortune. Bring your drum. You will find her in blue leggings, writhed around her trunk. She is home to many creatures like the purple lemur and the golden palm civet. Green fleecy ferns grow at her feet, and the fury and feathery alike live on her branches and under her leaves. She has been waiting to dance with someone for quite some time." Reyan, excited but concerned, asks Mr. Pitcher, "I don't know how to dance but I can play my drum." "Don't worry machan, you will do fine and she will dance." The plant predicts. "Be on your way, friends...

Kami begins by singing his sing-along-green song. "I want to be green, I prefer unseen, let's dance on the scene." He brings out the violin and his fiddle tail. The smaller plants begin to expand their roots and sway their leaves in a lateral direction toward the dam. Some movement in the soil below is felt under Kami's mitts. Further along, mid-way to the river and dam, cunning Cassie carries along in a cat-like tune: "Count with me, one, two, three, dance to the beat. I'm Cassie the cat, come along and count with me-dance to the beat." And, the canopy floor below her begins to undulate like underground waves in the fauna.

Further along, Reyan hikes around the outskirts of the dam in the dense foliage and finds an enormous tree with a gray disposition and beautiful blue skirt that elegantly wraps around her trunk. *This must be her, he wonders. No other trees have blue leggings like this one.* "Hello, are you Sharma? You wanna dance?" He plants his feet near her blue coat and begins to beat on his drum. "Dun, dun, bum, dun, bum. Ba, da, da, da." The blue coat on her trunk begins to reverberate to the beat. "dun, dun, bum, bum, ba, da, da, da." Then blue butterflies fly off her trunk and land on her trunk again to the beat of his drumming.

Reyan takes a break from drumming and then stands up straight and tall. He lifts his arms, gathers all the light under the canopy, and swings his arms from left to right toward the dam. Nothing happens at first, but he tries it again. He gathers the scatters of light and sways his arms from left to right and begins to feel the ground vibrate. Then he beats on his drum again and again. Sharma comes to life-rolling her roots and swaying her branches-she is dancing with Reyan. He keeps dancing, swaying, and drumming. Reyan cries out, "Mr. Pitcher sent me to dance with you. We need your help!" The giant tree mumbles, "What would a little-boy like you want with an old, tired, tree-like me?" "Well, of course, to dance with you, Ms. Sharma. I brought my drum and rays of light!" Sharma pauses, "I see that machan, you were blessed by a god, most likely Shiva.! I can feel your light charm when you flow your arms from right to left, my leaves pull with you, and when you beat your drum, I feel the vibrations in my roots." Reyan giggles and shares more, "We uncovered monkey business in the rainforest. Mr. Raji and his sapphire mine are diverting water from the river into a large dam." Sharma replies, "That must be why my leaves have been shriveling and my roots have been itchy." Reyan adds, "The streams and creeks are drying up and my parent's coffee plantation is running out of the water on their terraces. The beans are acidic and dry." Sharma reassures Reyan, "Ah, machan, Mr. Pitcher was wise to send you to me, let us dance under the canopy to the beat of the drum!" Reyan keeps beating on the drum:

Bum, bum, bum, bum,
Bum, bum.
Bum, bum, bum, bum

Sharma's roots expand and her butterflies continue to flutter above her trunk and back onto her trunk. The whole canopy expands with a super large underground lattice growing and contracting to a rhythmic beat. Reyan sways his arms further toward the dam. Cassie and Kami show up and join in on the dance.

Sharma sings,

Whether it's shady or sunny, you might like to know-I lack money, la, de, da. I lack money, la, de, da.

My leaves are green but not that kind, you see, I lack money, la, de, da. I used to believe this is all they would see, I lack money. Dance, if you will, with me,
I ease time and bring good fortune
I lack money.

Lakshmi has blessed me
I lack money...
Dance along with me, friends and family

When you invite me to dance

We can break this bad trance
I lack money.

Cassie, Kami, and Reyan keep dancing with Sharma. The fauna floor below them swells and pulses, undulating toward the dam. When the wave lattice reaches the dam, cracks in the cement begin to grow. Enlarged roots erupt through the surface of the cement and entangle around the broken dam. More and more cracks develop then, finally, the whole structure crumbles to the ground. Huge waves of dam water crash down onto Mr. Raji's mine, filling the ledges and caves. Blue sapphires spill out of their sluices and storage containers and sink to the bottom of the river that springs back to life. The diversion of water to the mines slowly re-route through the coffee plantation and fill the old grooves and canals of the terraces. The plants below the destruction begin to fill with moisture and life as they drink from the ground water.

Back at Blue Spirit Coffee Co., Jyoti and Krishi see the irrigation canals revive again. They are amazed and surprised at this suddenly natural turn of events. *They look up as if Vishnu himself broke a dam in the sky.* Meanwhile, Reyan, Cassie, and Kami return to thank Mr. Pitcher for his wisdom. He greets them with a victorious smile. "Machan and fellow creatures, we must not tell anyone about how we restored the water supply to the forest. The power lies in the beat of the drum and the light of the day, and you, machan, have saved the day!"

Reyan returns to the plantation with a sense of accomplishment and friends that would always be there for him. He keeps his heroic adventure a secret but decides to ask his parents for a civet cat. "We must get a golden palm civet," he pleads. "Why should we?" Jyoti asks. Reyan brings them his National

Geographic, "Look at this story I found in the magazine about golden palm civet cats. They poop out choice coffee beans that sell for three times as much as our blue bean variety." Reyan encourages. "Ok, machan, I will ask your father, but you will have to look after it if she says yes." He waits until the next day and tips off Cassie that his dad may set a cat trap full of ripe coffee cherries and be ready to splurge. Reyan is happy to offer Cassie a job, "Keep an eye out for a coffee bean trap and go for it, Cashie! My father will trap you, catch you, and you can work with me selling Cashie coffee beans." Cassie's eyes show dollar signs again.

Three days later, the family wakes up to a civet cat trapped in a cage. Reyan gets his parents and approaches his new employee-friend arrangement with a handful of choice red and yellow coffee cherries. He opens the trap door and hands Cassie some cherries. Cassie jumps up on Reyan and continues to chew the beans like she has for years. Amazed, his parents look in shock at how well the exotic jungle cat takes to their vitiligo son. Krishi for the first time in many months shares a proud moment with his son, "Reyan, my son, I am thrilled with your business sense and, not to mention, your charm with animals." Reyan's soul fills with joy and a new sense of satisfaction on where he belongs in his family and their savory mission to share inspirational coffee with the world. Jyoti hugs her son and husband and joins her family together for a big embrace.

Once again, they look up into the mystical blue and smile at Vishnu.

WELCOME TO HICKSVILLE

BY PORSHA STENNIS

When I was eight, I could never tell the difference between gunshots and firecrackers. My ears could never rip apart whether the loud pops ringing off into the midnight air meant drop to my knees and press my body into the carpet, until my skin was engraved with vague patterns, or simply gaze outside the front window and watch sparks fly. We, me and Mama and Noah, were still living on Creek Road, a strip of shit known as The Trail when I finally recognized the difference.

Our 'humble abode' was hiked up on the corner facing an abandoned playground that belonged to the part-time dope boys, raccoons, and oftentimes street rats. And I mean real street rats, probably almost as large as the ones that roam New York City. I've never been there before, but I can imagine their long tails being what gives them away, too, when they curl underneath rocks and dig into the Earth's dirt. The dope boys here in Hicksville, North Carolina probably ain't that different from theirs either.

Just like the dudes from *The Wire*, they've always seemed real intimidating in their oversized jeans sagging beneath their waistline and large bubble coats, sweatshirts, or white t-shirts depending on the season. Whenever I would peek out of the corners of our front window, I'd see at least three of them, silk durags draping their shoulders and hands stuffed in their jeans, just standing around the swing sets watching the block. They were like mutes, never seen any of them talk, only slap hands with whoever they came in contact with. Rather than words exchanged, they shared money and bags of drugs.

Mama caught me sitting on the arm of the couch once while I was watching them. I had the shades pried open enough to reveal my identity, letting them know that I knew what they were doing, though it wasn't on purpose and I actually didn't have the slightest clue.

"Boy, if you don't find some business!" she shouted and grabbed me by the collar of my shirt, yanking me so hard from my seat that my neck ached for weeks. *"Those men out there kill to protect themselves, and here you are just sitting up here staring them down like a hawk. They got enough police on their asses as is."*

That night, while I lay in bed with my pillow smothering my face to block out the rays of the moon that slithered through the blinds, I heard what sounded like balloons being popped; some at once, making the sound brasher than any ol' pop, and back-to-back, right after the next with no breaks in between like there were balloons lined up in a row. Something about it didn't sound like the fireworks the boys in the trailer behind us used to throw against the concrete or flare up into the air. These were deeper, more hollow. I knew for sure what it was when a bullet shattered the same front window I gazed out earlier that day, and when it lodged in the wall sprinkling plaster down on the dirty brown carpet of our small living room.

I think that was when mama figured my innocence had been shattered too, but now that I look back, I think that was the night and moment something in her broke. Her gray eyes never looked the same, that streak of silver that glittered like marbles in the sun was gone. They darkened after the police came to our home and clipped photos of every crevice and corner they figured was evidence, after they wrote up an extensive report, and eventually arrested the men who they assumed did the crime.

After that we were forced to move out of The Trail due to threats.

Mama used to always say, *"It's not safe 'round here anymore. Not for anyone."* But what she really meant was it wasn't safe for our family.

Even besides Mama swearing the men across the street now had a hit out on us, we weren't your average trio. See, Mama was white. She looked just like Farrah Fawcett, except her hair didn't bounce like hers, her skin didn't often glow with the shade of pink like hers. She was Farrah traced with lines of age and years of stress.

Unlike Mama, I was darker, and my hair was a lot thicker than hers. There was no bounce in sight whenever I picked out my braids, it was stiff unless drenched in water. Then it curled up, not as loose as Noah's curls but close enough. Noah looked more like mama and if we're being real, I was the oddball who made us stand out.

Growing up on The Trail, or better yet, all over the outskirts of this small North Carolina city loaded with nine-hundred black folks and the other couple of hundred whites - I knew *something* about our family was off. I peeped it in the way people would look when they saw us coming, locked and loaded, hip to hip like our very own version of the Huxtables. They'd quickly glance with a smile, look away as if there was nothing to see, then almost break their necks doing a double take. Because every block we lived on - whether filled with trailers, or two-bedroom apartments on Cherry Avenue, or where we are now living in our own house on Belmore Drive - was mixed with different shades, I figured what was wrong with us wasn't the fact that Mama was paler than both Noah and me. I honestly thought it was because we were obviously poor.

Mama was never able to buy me brand new outfits until she took on three jobs. I was twelve by then and during that time, Mama made me the man of the house. She figured I was old enough to walk home from school, make sure Noah was bathed and fed before his bedtime of eight o'clock, then get myself ready for bed too. The reward in return for doing everything she typically did for us and staying out of trouble was sometimes a new shirt, sometimes a pair of jeans, and other times, some shoes. Nothing was ever name brand and always your standard pieces, but it was a lot better than the thrift store fits and hand me down garments she was gifted from coworkers.

Now, as I sit on our porch, no longer an adolescent, but quickly approaching adulthood, no longer a stranger to those confused looks or stares between racks at the Food Lion from strangers completely intrigued, I realize we were and still are odd because of the times, because of the place. Wasn't nothing normal about a single white woman raising two black boys in the South, or at least not in The Ville.

The Ville was everything she didn't want me to know, but everything I needed to know.

Before me, outside of my mind wandering back from the past, was a gold, beat down Cavalier parked in the middle of the street. The passenger side window was cracked just enough for me to hear Justin Timberlake harmonizing *cry me a river* while the horn blaring in the background eclipsed the Timbaland composed beat.

It was Michelle, my companion in crime and karaoke partner. If you let Mama tell it, she is secretly my girlfriend too. She lives ten minutes away in a neighborhood called Lafayette Park and even though it isn't as nice as Edgewood where I stay, which still isn't 'top tier' either, it's a come up from The Trail. The houses are smaller than ours, usually only one floor off the ground accompanied by a covert basement. The tiles of the houses that stretch along every block for nearly a mile are peeling if not already fallen off.

Landscapes don't exist.

Front yards around these parts are covered in mostly dirt and dead grass, and the bushes never survive the constant warmth because those who own the houses can't afford the upkeep.

Michelle's house is owned by her gran, and before her gran, her great gran, and before that, you get the idea. I'd like to think the reason for them living there all this time was due to funds, because if Mama finessed us into Edgewood then so could they, but rather it was a given. History kept them rooted in the same house for as long as I've known Michelle, since we were ten years old, and it would keep them there forever.

We aren't much alike and that could be why we click so well; opposites attract and a balance is made. She is everything I'm not - outspoken, rebellious, and brave. I'm book smart, she's more street smart and that gives strangers the idea that Michelle is older than seventeen. Though we both have a license, Michelle is the only one allowed to drive and because we both only have two classes, we need to take in order to grad-uate from Wiggins come Friday, she also picks me up most mornings, like today.

"Hurry up, Toby!" Michelle yelled as she leaned over the console to get a better look at me dressed in whatever FUBU paraphernalia I had washed last night. "We ain't got all day!"

"Yeah, yeah, yeah." I mumbled and quickly skipped down

the steps. By the time I made it to the bottom I heard the hinges of the screen door squeak and the patter of soft footsteps along the wooden floorboard behind me. It could have only been Mama since Noah was still in our room, playing video games and eating pop tarts, and I knew for sure when she cleared her throat.

"You gone?" she asked as I barely turned my head around, getting a glimpse of her face. Mama had her arms crossed over her chest and her lips pursed, but her eyes were looking behind me, locked to Michelle.

"Yes, ma'am," I nodded...

"Mhm, well, don't be out all day." she muttered. "And stay out of trouble."

For a second I couldn't tell whether she was speaking to me or Michelle since her eyes had yet to shift to me, not even for a second.

"Oh, we will, Ms. Sadie!" Michelle shouted back, and my chest ached as I heard sarcasm drip from her words. Mama never cared for Michelle's slick mouth, not now, and not when we were younger. She always said it would lead her to a world of trouble and yet her world was Hicksville. So, weren't we all in trouble?

"Let's go, Toby!" Michelle yelled once again and aggressively honked her horn, even though I was approaching the car...

Justin was now crooning *Senorita*, Pharrell made the complimentary beat.

"Bye, Mama," I waved farewell as I hopped inside while Michelle wasted no time pressing her foot onto the gas, and sped off to the main intersection.

At the corner she glanced both ways, whisking in the array of cars flying down the street that became a highway after many miles. Her fingers tapped against the rubber steering wheel cover as she sang along to the repetitive lyrics she knew by heart. Michelle hit every other note, better than Justin even, while I shifted my hips and pushed the seat back, letting my legs stretch out.

Michelle finally cut the wheel when the light turned green and made a sharp turn onto what we knew as Burling Road. On the outskirts were mostly trees and homes hidden behind them, then before we reached the parking lot of our school, there were grocery stores at every other exit, a dollar store here, Sally's there, your favorite fast-food restaurants beside them, a Waffle House, and our favorite morning spot, Duck Donuts.

Michelle always tried to grab a dozen from the one near her house before she picked me up, getting anything from their French Toast, Strawberry Shortcake, Chocolate Caramel Crunch, and Cookies and Crème. They were not only diabetes rolled into dough but on the expensive side, too, and yet somehow Michelle and I managed to put our money from side jobs together just so we could kick our feet up on the dashboard before the bell rang and swallow two down. We always drank milk with them, I preferred regular, she loved chocolate, and I always silently thanked God I wasn't at school all day since I more than likely had a case of the shits soon after.

"Your mom needs to loosen up a bit. No one likes a party pooper," Michelle teased as she reached her arm out to grab my shoulder then gave it an ecstatic squeeze. "Can you believe it? We're almost done, Toby! In two hours, we'll officially be done with high school!"

"Wait," my back perked up from the seat as did my head as I scanned the street. "Where are we going?"

Crickets, static, all the weird things you hear in the middle of silence persisted. And silence between us wasn't normal. Let me take that back, silence for Michelle wasn't normal. She always had something to say, and though most times I hated her unsolicited opinions, I needed it now. If I were lucky, she'd slap me and tell me I was being dumb, then I'd know she at least cared.

We pulled into the Amoco and Michelle parked beside one of the many empty gas pumps. I chewed into my bottom lip as she unlocked her seatbelt and flung it over her shoulder. Flinching came as second nature once she abruptly turned in her seat and looked over at me with her arm stretched behind the headrest.

"You're more than this place, Tobias." Michelle began as I sighed and rubbed at the hair along my temple. "You can't just throw those opportunities away. What's going on?"

"Nothing, it's just jitters."

"This ain't just jitters. Is this about the money? I can help you apply for more scholarships," she rambled. "Maybe you can do that work study stuff the counselors always tal-"

"No," I quickly inserted. "I just don't think college was ever my option, but my mama's. I don't even know what I want to study and what if I get there and never find what I'm good at or what I enjoy? I don't even know much of who I am. It would all be a waste."

"Well...I never thought about that," she mumbled, eyes wandering out the front windshield. "But I'm sure you can figure that out somewhere that isn't *here*. This place is a trap."

"What is one more year going to do if you've lived here for seventeen already?"

Her mouth hung wide.

"Have we not been struggling since we came out our mothers' crotches? Have we not dreamed of going places outside of North Carolina's borders? We can barely make it to Greensboro," she snapped. "You have the ticket to get out. Is this something you really want to debate?"

"Well, I did ask, so..."

Michelle rolled her eyes before the sound of the door unlocking clicked.

"You know, one day those are going to get stuck."

"I've been rolling them for seventeen years now, what will one more day do?"

I couldn't help but chuckle as the tables turned and Michelle refrained from saying anything else. Instead, she dug into the pocket of her jeans and handed me a crumpled ten-dollar bill. I snatched it from her hand and popped the door open, then got out, making sure to slam it shut. With one glance at the thrifted Casio watch on my wrist, I noted we only had a few minutes before the bell rang and quickly picked up my pace. I unfolded the bill and rolled it over my knee, hoping some of the kinks disappeared. Once it was presentable, I jogged to the small convenience store and paid the cashier.

When Michelle only needed gas, and she only needed gas when I was with her, she refused to get out. So as a matter of routine, I made my way back to the pump and began filling the tank. My fingers drummed against the roof of her car as I stared off into space, taking in the same scenery I'd known all my life.

There was nothing new, Hicksville rarely saw new infrastructure or businesses, new playgrounds, new schools, new people, new nothing. Just the same ol' same ol'. It was comfortable, predictable. I never knew anything different than what I saw and that brought me comfort, but comfort was also unexciting. It was repetitive and even exhausting. It was like living the same day over and over again, and the circumstances, to say the least, never got better.

Maybe Michelle had a point.

I grappled with the thought until the horn of the car grabbed my attention. I leaned down and peeked into the window of Michelle's backseat as she nodded her head toward her window. For a second it was lost on me what she was getting to. Did she want me to wipe her windows down while I was out here, too? When she realized, from the ripples in my forehead, that I had no clue what her nod meant, Michelle pointed her finger out the car instead.

Across the street a group of guys sat on the hood of their cars, a beatdown Buick Roadmaster and LeSabre, just outside one of the few liquor stores on this side of town. Unlike near The Trail, if you found a liquor store within even a five miles radius you were lucky. Closer to our school everything was slightly nicer, cleaner, quieter, and dare I say, safer.

But these men. I marveled at how unworried they seemed, minding their business, finding something to joke at as they occupied their own world, one that seemed so separate from the one around them. Clouds of smoke swarmed their faces as they shouted over the chorus of DMX's *What's My Name* blasting from the windows of one of their cars. The scene wasn't unusual, even this early in the morning.

As I said before, I was used to this, these were the dudes who settled somewhere in the middle of the spectrum. There were the corner boys on one end, the extreme, then there were ones like me, the ones who were scared away from trouble and had a 'promising' future. But in between there were these guys. Not so much troublemakers, but instead those who might not have the options I have and wouldn't choose the option those on the extreme believed was their only. They are just there, existing in what exists for them and not creating something different out of it.

"Stay here and you'll be just like them," Michelle hissed. "That's Leon over there, you know."

He was a few years older than us, graduated three years ago when we were freshmen and never left the city. From what I last remember, he worked at a burger joint and has a daughter on the way.

"He's not that bad off," I mumbled, and from the way he was dressed, he really didn't look like it. His white sneakers were the sharpest things on that side of the street. He had freshly creased jeans hanging from his hips and the red Rocawear shirt was one from their latest collection. I knew because I had window-shopped it my damn self.

"Sure," Michelle scoffed. "Keep playing stupid."

I groaned and looked away to the pump, checking how much of the ten dollars was left. Just as the pump slowed to a crawl at $9.75, the music seemed to dissolve into the air becoming whispers and my head swung over my shoulder seeing why.

Like a master puppeteer was in control, everything seemed to proceed at the same slow pace as the pump inching up to the 10-dollar click off point. Everything was in slow motion. The attention of everyone looking on like bystanders shifted and became stuck. Leon and his friends' eyes followed the white Ford pickup truck turning inside the parking lot and that eventually made itself comfortable right beside the LeSabre. One by one, as its engine continued to roar without a body inside stirring and exiting its doors, Leon and his friend's bodies raised from their cars and like the heads in whack-a-mole-, their necks stretched up, hoisting their heads high. They stood like toy soldiers minus the salutes with their hands stuffed in their pockets or arms crossed defiantly over their chests.

"Let's go," Michelle said, though nothing about her body language agreed. She was stuck just like I was.

I swallowed the lump that had suddenly gathered in my throat and watched what now officially felt the climax of a movie.

The red, blue, and white flag hanging off the back of the truck, graciously fluttering in the wind, had stolen the show from Leon's shoes. The stars crossing over each other into the mark of an X could be recognized anywhere by anyone. It was a distorted version of the American flag. It was an emblem and most times folks steered away from it, but not these guys.

These guys with Leon were something heroic because they drew near it like a magnet.

A heavyset white man donning the typical uniform most folks who carried the flag wore - washed jeans, a short-sleeved plaid shirt, and a cap or cowboy hat - finally hopped out of the driver's side. He marched into the store as they glared him down.

How could anyone ignore the daggers they were shooting?

Once inside, Leon rushed over to the man's truck and snatched the flag down, and before I could blink he was stomping it, smothering it deeper and deeper into the gravel. One of his friend's followed suit and even went as far as showing his disdain by spitting on it while another let his can of beer bleed onto it. Together they all kicked it around like a soccer ball while the rest of the group turned the music back up and laughed loudly at their antics. Just as I found humor in what they were doing, admiring them for their boldness and bravery, I also felt my breath hitch as my stomach stiffened.

I was afraid.

Suddenly the time on my watch wasn't just the countdown for Michelle and me, but for Leon and his friends, too. I didn't want us to be late and for them to get caught. Everyone knew what guys who carried that thing were capable of.

"Alright, come on. Let's go!" Michelle yelled, blowing her horn again. I made sure her tank was secured then walked over to my door and inched my leg inside. The rest of me couldn't pull away. "I'm sure they've done this before now, Toby. They'll be fine."

After a few more moments of them destroying the piece of fabric until it was practically waste, the man exited from the store, catching them as they hurried away from the act and dived back into their cars. I couldn't make out what all he yelled as he rushed over to the cab of his truck and reached inside.

"Seriously," Michelle's voice was a lot less aggressive, shaky even. "Tobias, get in the car. We should really go...now!"

When he pulled his arm back, his hand gripped a rifle that had been laying across the front seat. That was when my eyes broadened and my heart stopped. I swallowed hard and again and again until he aimed the muzzle toward their cars speeding out of the parks and hiked behind them as he continued to yell.

Michelle gripped my jeans and yanked me inside. I fell into the passenger's seat and fumbled with the handle of the door as she immediately pulled off and at the light just outside the gas station, turned onto the road, heading back in the direction to school. I peered back through the rear window, seeing the man finally lower his gun and reach down to pick up what was left of his precious flag.

Silence riddled the moment. I was a mime, nothing but a blank stare summed up how I felt. What was once a thrill, a distraction, entertainment, somehow played out into a nightmare.

"A lot," Michelle stated firmly as she adjusted the volume of her radio. "A whole lot can happen."

* * *

We had already smacked two potholes before Mama decided to dodge them. By then her effort didn't matter because her back tire had blown out and the frame of her old Chevy Impala was wobbling from side to side like a pregnant woman in her last trimester. The windows were cracked just enough for me to hear the air fizzle out, it sounded like a snake hissing in heat.

Our bodies staggered as she dodged nothing, nothing but air. She dodged air instead of potholes and until the front bumper kissed the curb and sank into the dirt. I tucked my bottom lip between my teeth. From the corner of my eye, I could see her tossing her hands in the air before they landed on the steering wheel and tightly clamped its lumpy edges.

"Got dammit," she cursed. "That can't be no good. Can't be." And she was right.

Mama wasn't no mechanic or Jiffy Lube employee. Like Michelle, she always made me pump her gas, and I was sure that was the only thing related to cars, besides driving them into holes, that she knew how to do. Mama was a cleaner; she kept spaces spic and span, spotless, tidy, and comfortable. She even kept her car clean, but anything else was foreign to her.

"Well..."

I knew what was coming next, what she was ready to ask me and at times like this, I wondered what my pops would do? I mean, I don't know who he is or nothing, but I'd imagined he'd crack the driver's side door open and stretch his long legs, covered with macho hair, outside into the approaching heat-wave of summer. He'd hike to the trunk, and from the passenger's seat where I sat in a rented suit swallowing every part of me, tie firm around my neck, I'd grin as he would wave me over to join him. Excitement would lull me from my seat. Inside the trunk would be a spare tire and we'd both slap our hands together, rub our palms as we revved up the strength to clasp the tire's ridges, let the dirt sink into our fingerprints, and tug and tug until we pull it out and toss it to the concrete.

"You grab that toolbox and roll up your sleeves, hear me? We got work to do."

For some reason, I hoped he came from a long line of men who liked to get their hands filthy. You know, those blue-collar men who only know the creases and curves of an ironed uniform, the men who wear their names proudly above their left breast and are always ready to fix something.

"Now, hand me that red box snuggled in that corner," he'd point to the right of me and I'd reach out with one hand, doing as told, but only before he stops me. *"Easy, youngin'. It's heavy, so you betta lift it with ya legs and not your back. Or you'll be sorry. Ya know, way before my daddy up and left my maw and me to move across the country, he'd let me help bring in all the groceries and when I got older, I started lugging in heavier stuff. I was a man then, so I thought. Until I pulled something in my back at fourteen. He warned me plenty, told me to lift with my legs, but I ain't know what he was talking about. So, I did what I thought all the men do."*

Here is where I'd laugh because something about this would strike me as funny.

"Boy, when I tell you to listen, do it. Don't wanna be silly like me and in pain."

I'd imagine I'd be just like him. Not knowing a thing about whatever knowledge he was babbling about at the moment, but maybe not so much silly and in pain, because unlike him I'd watch closely. I guess I get that from Mama, she notices everything. I'd watch as he would carefully take the toolbox from my grasp, lift it to his chest just as he squatted enough to pull it higher and from the trunk. With so much grace, as if the toolbox was a delicate feather, my pops would stroll a few feet away and place it by the tire.

Mama turned her head and looked over at me, wearing the same suit and tie. Not from a window at the rear of the car, but from across the seat, she looked into my eyes. She was waiting. Her bright eyes something like those of a wolf, watched and waited. She waited for me to be the man, yet again. The man I never had in my life, the thing I didn't know how to be. I shut my eyes, hoping maybe my imagination would run rampant and I'd learn from pops. He'd take me through it, step by step. Maybe he had a handbook or just some wise words from his own father. I squeezed my eyes tighter, but nothing happened.

"Well," she repeated, this time harsher. "How you expect to get to this graduation of yours if you're not gonna get out and see what needs to be fixed?"

I shrugged as she chuckled and shook her head.

"You better figure it out then."

That was what I was good at, figuring things out on my own. It was way easier than asking her because Mama made my problems, my questions a Rubik's Cube; impossible to resolve.

I reached my hand over to the door to clutch the knob between my fingertips then forced it open. I got out of the car and quickly shimmied my blazer from my shoulders. It fell to my waist and down to my wrists before I placed it on the roof and sighed. Sweat had gathered underneath my armpits and dampened the material of my buttoned-up shirt tucked neatly into my pants. I wanted to rip every single article of clothing from my body, it was so hot. I was so frustrated; we were officially late.

The skin of my forehead began to perspire, beads trickled down my temple, but a thin breeze from the shade saved me. It brushed against my features and swathed my neck like a silk durag. It was enough to calm me, to slip under me and haul me to the auditorium two miles away. It was enough until it wasn't. Mama honked her horn. She reminded me to come back to reality.

I walked back to the trunk she had conveniently popped open for me and grabbed the large metal piece whose name I couldn't remember, another tool that looked significant, and the spare tire itself. I hauled it all over to the one that had flattened and tried to recall just how to change it.

Michelle and I were fourteen when her father spent weeks

inside her grandmother's garage fixing up the car she now calls her own. Most times we'd remain inside and try to ignore all the loud tools ringing off on the other side of the walls, but one day he invited us in. Not only did he show us how to change a tire but he taught us what certain buttons and switches were for and what certain lights meant. He even let Michelle drive around the block before he continued on to show us how to pump gas and all other simple things you should know when owning a vehicle. Little did she know, he was preparing her for now; for the times when she'd need to fix something that goes wrong and he wouldn't be there to assist. Little did I know, it was the one and only lesson I'd received from a male figure, one I'd need on the biggest day of my life.

He had prepared us both to save ourselves.

I squatted down and played around with the tools, wedging them into places that they best fit into. I shoved, twisted and even banged against the hubcap but nothing. The heat only intensified as I struggled and tried to ignore mama as she stared out of the window, watching me, but not helping. At this point I no longer wanted to go anywhere. I just wanted to sit along the side of the road and rest in the shade.

"You getting anything done down there?" Mama asked, and I nodded just to get her off my ass.

As she prepared to say something else, a siren sounded off, cutting her short. I was relieved, for one, that I was spared from her unnecessary commentary and maybe even thankful that they were coming to assist, but in that same breath I was even more nervous because what if it was just my luck the officer who got out assumed I was doing something other than failing to change my mother's tire.

The door slammed shut as I kept my head down and fiddled around with the same tools. I could hear footsteps behind me getting closer and, from the corner of my eye, the pace of the feet they belonged to slowed down and stopped just before me. I was trying not to look awkward, but it didn't matter because I felt it.

"Everything okay down here?"

"I caught a flat and it looks like neither of us know what to do," Mama blurted from the window. "I tell you about these roads."

The officer squatted down and cleared his throat, my head edged around toward him. He was much younger than I anticipated, nothing like the old white dudes with beer bellies hanging over the belt of their uniforms. His dark brown eyes, matching his dark brown hair, scanned me closely as he rolled his sleeves up his forearms.

"Where are you going all dressed up?" he asked. "And you're sweating out your suit like you stole something."

I cleared my throat as he took the metal piece from my hands and began properly placing the tools for the job.

"To my graduation."

"High school?"

I quickly nodded. "Yes sir," I peered down at the badge on his chest, *B. Dale*. "W-we're late now, b-but I'd still like to go."

"I bet. Well, I might be able to help." He signaled for me to scoot over and began switching out the tire, making it look so easy. "Don't I know you?"

I slowly shook my head.

Yes.

"No, I don't think so, s-sir."

"Hm," was all I received in return. "You look pretty familiar."

My brows tightened. I was lost on how to respond.

"You don't hang around over on Melrose? Near the public housing?"

"I-...I think you have me confused with someone else."

He pursed his lips and leaned down, getting a better view of one of the lug nuts.

"Maybe so. A lot of you people favor each other," he mumbled. *If the hair of my brows weren't completely enmeshed with my hairline by now, I'd be shocked.*

"That your mother?"

"Yes, that would be my mother," I grumbled. Something about the tone of his questions left me feeling as if he didn't believe anything I was saying and that he was only looking for a lie.

"Adopted?"

"Nope, he is all mine!" Mama shouted from the driver's seat and for the first time today I was thankful for it. "You all done there, officer? We'd really like to get going now. We don't want to miss them calling my eldest on that stage, now do we? He's in the top ten of his class."

The officer snickered and tossed the piece down before rubbing the dirt from his hands.

"No ma'am, we don't. You all are all set. Might want to toss this old tire."

"Will do," she said before sitting back into her seat.

"Uh, thank you, sir."

I hesitantly reached my hand out for a polite handshake, but instead he nodded and slapped his onto my shoulder, giving it a pinch. I looked down at its placement and the shadow of dirt that lingered.

"Mhm," he assured. "And cheers on the diploma. I'll be seeing you around I'm sure," his smirk was somewhat devious as he winked and turned around, retreating back to his wagon.

* * *

"We really have to teach you how to switch out a tire again," Michelle muttered as she leaned deeper into our half hug. She smiled ahead as her gran held up her disposable camera to her slanted eye. She counted down from five. "Even I know how to do that."

"We know you do."

"Say cheese!" Gran belted as her voice trembled with age.

"Cheese!"

"Not my fault you forgot," Michelle shot back. "You missed half of our graduation. Clearly this is life or death."

Gran captured another photo and then the shutter of Mama's OneStep instant camera flipped open, a light flashed and a perfect square framing the shadows of Michelle and I eased out from the front. We both shifted our bodies into another awkward pose, this one being us holding up the navy-blue caps with red and white tassels dangling from their centers into the air.

"Whatever, Elle," I gritted through another crooked smile. "I made it. That's all that matters, right?"

Michelle's arms immediately fell to her hips. She frowned over at me, just as she always does when she's dissatisfied with something I do or say that doesn't quite sit with her philosophy of life. Michelle wasn't like me, inhibited in a way, an introvert. So whenever I responded to her nonchalantly, without the passion or desire that gushed through her veins, she was disappointed. Her disappointment was one I could accept though. It was one out of love, one I knew she fleshed out because she cared or because she wanted me to be better. I never felt like it was from a place of disgust. It never felt like the disappointment from Mama.

"No, that is not all that matters. You came late with sweat and dirt all over your shirt because," she bit into her tongue as she glanced over at her gran and Mama, both busy swooning over the developed Polaroids. They were distracting, and enough for Michelle to stop spilling her opinion. "Never mind."

"Can we just go to Waffle House and get some food? I'm tired of this heat and the one's on this side of town have air conditioning."

"Is Ms. Sadie coming?"

I shook my head and looked back over to our guardians, just as Mama was walking toward the two of us.

"I need to head on back home and get some rest before my shift. You be in the house by eleven," She ordered as she pointed her finger my way. "Alright? And remember, Saturday nights I work my regular, and a half. Don't wait up."

"Yes ma'am."

Without a goodbye, an I love you, or even a be careful, Mama walked off and never once looked back.

"Your mother is like the wicked witch of the west of Hicksville."

"Elle..."

"What?" Her shoulders rose slightly and momentarily as she placed her cap back onto her hair that was slowly puffing up at the roots the longer we stood under the sun. Our complexions were both evening out with a tan. "I meant what I said. Besides, you live with her, you should know."

"But she's still my mother, and she's not that bad...all the time."

"Preach to another choir. And if that's what it's like to have a mother, then I don't ever want one."

Neither one of us knew what really happened to her mother.

Michelle grabbed my hand in hers and walked over to Gran who held a wide smile on her face. She leaned forward into

Michelle's chest, wrapped her arms around her back, then kissed her cheek before she spoke up...

"I'm proud of you, love bug. Now, stay out of trouble for the rest of the summer and you might just become my favorite grandchild."

I snickered at her comment while Michelle pursed her lips and stepped back from their embrace.

"Sure, Gran, sure. Now, let me take you back home before we go grab some food."

"Actually, baby. Go on and take me to The Florence. I'll get the receptionist that leaves at four to drop me off at home. You go and enjoy your big day."

"Is daddy getting out today or something?" Michelle's brow perked up. For years, her father had been in and out of rehab for his alcohol addiction. This was clearly a cycle they had both become accustomed to.

Gran's lips parted as she began to answer, but she stopped and shook her head as her eyes lowered.

"Not yet, baby. But soon."

Michelle had a thing about the word soon. It was never on time. It was earlier than later. It was never guaranteed, but yet it was. Soon was as flaky as the word came and she never wanted to be promised that.

"Okay, Gran." Michelle nodded forward, leading the way to their car. I watched as she had, again, within a few days' span become a version of herself I wasn't used to - inhibited and quiet. Something was on her mind that she couldn't quite formulate into words. I hadn't learned how to respond to that yet, but I was learning and figured in this instance she might have wanted to be reassured, of something. Anything.

I threw my arm over her shoulder as we continued to walk to her car.

"If it makes you feel better, I'm going. Don't know where yet, but I am. I just need to figure some things out."

"Well, that is relieving," she nearly whispered, nodding her head. "That Confederate flag change your mind?" Michelle smirked.

"They don't give you much of a choice but to leave, do they? You either."

"You're absolutely right...about me, I mean." Michelle laughed as I shook my head, just as we made it to her car. "But don't go letting anyone else chase you out of here. Ms. Sadie, poverty, nothing, and especially no Klan members. If you choose to leave, leave on your own terms. Leave for yourself."

"She's right," Gran agreed as she lowered herself into the passenger's side. A smile settled onto my lips as Michelle shrugged smugly and mirrored Gran's same movements. I took a final glance around at the parking lot and stored away this building as my first memory.

I said my first goodbye of the summer and never looked back.

SWEET AS SIN

BY DEREK WEINSTOCK

Erik's big idea was this: That what happened to food before it died was infinitely more important than what happened to it afterward. I can't say I liked the way he went about experimenting, though.

I came home one day and his desk had been cleared of his recipes and cookbooks and sitting there was a fish tank, in which an unhappy, fat trout swam sad little circles. He hadn't seen me in a long time, and when I came in he started kissing me deeply, but when I broke it off to ask about the fish, he forgot about anything else except explaining it.

"It's my thesis," he said. "I think it's going to change the fucking world."

The fish turned back and forth slowly, and stared blankly at us.

"I've been adding sugar water to the tank, slowly, over time. Eventually, I'll cook it with a sauce, serve it, and it'll be fantastic."

"Is it, uh, legal?"

"Not technically. But those laws are so fucking stupid. Like, you can boil a lobster alive, but you can't do this?"

"I guess."

It seems hard to believe, after everything, but that was the only conversation that we ever had about it. The fish was there for a month, breathing in the sweetened water painfully. I watched Erik take it out of the tank with his hands and looked away as he killed it and gutted it on the kitchen table. Even then, we didn't talk about what he was doing, though I could tell he was excited. I can't even watch him cook a whole lobster. I can't stand the sight of living—well, not living, but obviously once alive—animals being cooked. But Erik loved cooking, and I loved him. I met him in high school, and I loved him then, even though I once cheated on him with another boy. When we went to college, we wanted to live together for the whole thing (being with him was the only thing I liked about college, which to me seemed babyish and cloying, a luxury for rich kids afraid of life).

We lied to the administration, saying we were only friends and signed up for the gender-neutral housing option. Through the whole first year the RAs knew what was up, but they were too nervous to tell anyone. We moved to an out-of-school apartment the next year. I paid for it. The next year, Erik would pay. That last year, when we got the fish, I don't remember. I think it was me.

Erik took the fish out of the oven and dusted the outside with a couple of spices I didn't recognize. He mixed a sauce in a ceramic bowl with a fork, and made us each a plate, sauce on the side. He grinned at me.

"First bite without the sauce."

My mother used to say, "Sweet as sin."

After we finished eating, we made love on the bed. Erik was confident, victorious. I imagined myself as one of Genghis

Khan's concubines. I don't know where the fantasy came from, maybe I was studying him at the time.

But we were full and happy. I think I was happy. I didn't think about happiness much, at the time. I was running on autopilot, being true to the things I'd always thought about myself. I needed food to eat. I needed a bed to sleep in. And like I needed those things, I needed Erik.

Part of it was the weed. I was smoking a lot of weed at the time, two or three joints a day, and when I was high I would be happy. Little things would amuse me, little things would make me excited, nothing could get me down. One day, after going to class high, I came back, and there were two fish tanks. In one was a monstrous king crab, and in the other a boneless eel. These, to me, were not like the fish had been. Looking at them, I felt terrible about what Erik was doing, and I felt that they were complicit. I thought of them like a loving wife thinks of a teenage seductress; they had corrupted him with their flesh. I hated them, and life for giving birth to their races, and they hated me as well, behind their walls of plexiglass.

I said nothing to Erik of my hatred, but couldn't keep from manifesting it in small ways. I refused to undress in front of them, and took to wearing a bathrobe during the eight-step trip from shower to bed. I put off making love when I could, and would only do so under the sheets, despite that it was summer. When Erik asked me to feed them, I nodded, but I would not. I hated to watch them eat, the eel's quick, targeted bites, the crab's mandibles chewing. A couple times, when I was drunk and alone, I added dish soap into their tanks, adding poison to Erik's exquisitely crafted mixture of fresh water, brine, and tasty things. Picture me in my robe, like the evil queen, unwilling to share her king even with his beloved child. When I thought of myself like that, it wasn't so bad. It had some history behind it.

This is not to say that I wanted them gone. I hated them, reviled them, feared them. But I would guiltily dream about the quality of that fish, the first one. I couldn't believe how much I found myself missing that taste, the sweetness built into the flesh itself. Nothing came close to it, nothing we had lost. Not the sex, not the liberation of being naked in my own home, not even looking at Erik without fear. Because I was afraid of him. But I was happy to be.

I came home one night from History of Medicine, a rare class that I liked a lot (because of the future doctors, male and female, with their odd, permanent seriousness. When they experienced the hell of residency, they would learn, by necessity, to have fun. Just to make it through those long months). I was not high, and I went looking for my stash in the mess our room had become. I heard a voice from behind me.

"Don't move. Don't you dare move."

I froze, half bent over, sifting through a small pile of clothes.

"Stand up. Just don't turn around."

I experienced his commands dreamily, and found myself thinking about who he was. Probably a robber. Probably not a rapist. I wondered if he even had a knife.

"Where do you keep the money, bitch?" A faint buzz of anger went through my head. *You're* the bitch, I thought. You don't even have a knife.

"You should get out of here," I said. "My boyfriend will be back soon. Then you're fucked."

"Shut up! Where's the money?" The same tone for both. Did he even want to know? Or was he just re-establishing our roles, him: scary robber, me: scared woman. I knew then what to say.

"You've got to go, kid." I turned, looked at him in his eyes. He was maybe sixteen years old, wearing a black hoodie. He was so afraid, it made him beautiful. Adorable. He held something in his pocket, but I no longer cared what it was.

"You have to go and never come back. When my boyfriend comes home he'll kill us both, just from you being here, just from you seeing me. He's done it before."

He was confused and he was angry, but his fear was swimming up from the depths of his mind, the devouring mother, come to swallow them whole.

"You need to run, boy. Run away from this place. You need to find somewhere else to rob. And you need to do it now. Because he's due home any minute."

"Shut up." He was almost whispering now.

"He's not far away." I allowed myself a smile, cruel and insane. "He's downstairs, with his friend."

I allowed a moment for him to speak and he said nothing, only a slight squeak of breath.

"I'm going to scream, now. If I scream, you may as well do what you want with me, because we'll both be dead." Overdramatic. But it worked.

He didn't even look at me. He turned and he left. Fast and clumsy. Just to scare him, because I hated him and I pitied him, I opened my mouth and screamed. The sound was painful and livid and mocking, and it went on for a very long time. Then I laughed, and the laughing hurt my throat and didn't satisfy like the scream. I sat down on the bed and waited for Erik. I decided not to tell him about anything.

Erik and I sat up that night and watched the fish tanks like a TV screen. I was half-hidden under the sheets, staring out like a kid afraid of monsters. To my surprise, I was more afraid of them now than I was before the burglary. He watched them passively, hungrily, like a farmer chewing a stalk of wheat.

"Tell me what you put in there with them."

"*That* one has lemon and white wine, and I add a tiny

amount of non-dairy creamer every two days. The plants growing there are lemongrass. Did you know it could grow underwater? And also a type of seaweed that's supposedly like catnip to these things." And indeed, I had seen it playing there, coiling up its scaly body around the leaves.

"What about him?"

"For that one it's less about the water. I feed him beef, raw hamburger, you know. There's no shelter in the tank, because when they hide in crevices, they get rigid and tough. Most people don't notice, but that's because they kill them the wrong way."

"How will you kill them?"

He exhaled in thought.

"I'll add morphine to the water. That way their muscles won't firm up. I'll probably start gutting them while they're still asleep."

"Erik?"

"What?"

"What would happen if you let them go?"

"Let them go, like, in the ocean?"

"Yeah."

"I'm not raising them to survive."

"Yeah. I know." A pause. "When will we eat them?"

"Maybe in a month."

"Okay."

"Erik?"

"Yeah?"

Then all of a sudden tiredness took me. I fell asleep quickly and finally, a dead fish drifting into black-blue depths.

The days became one gray cloud, afterward. The next morning I was tired, and played sick like when I was eight. I sat in my bed, lying to my professors over email, watching the tanks. The next day, I woke up and I was still tired.

Erik had me scared, though I could no longer tell if it was something he was doing, or it was all in my head. When I told him I wanted to spend Christmas break with my parents he said, "Oh. I thought we would spend it together," and I canceled my plans to travel. When I began hanging out with my plug, he said "It makes me uncomfortable," and I bought my weed elsewhere.

I continued poisoning the fish, more and more often dropping dish soap and detergent into their tanks, but I worried he would catch me at it. I became an expert poisoner. Erik was making their lives miserable and delicious; I was murdering them, slowly and painfully, for no reason at all. I hid the dust inside of pills in the neat little balls of ground beef. I dripped bleach from an eyedropper into their tanks.

Erik circled a day on the calendar in red.

One day, I found a bag full of my clothes on the stairs and was unable to remember which of us had packed it.

I went to CVS and bought too much rat poison. After all, I didn't even know if it would work on them.

Three days away from the day Erik had circled, he went out partying with some friends. I stood there, above the tanks, looking down at them because they couldn't look back up at me that way. I stared down. The water was slightly murky, dusty. Slowly, I opened a bottle and poured it out into the one on my left. I opened another bottle. I looked back at the eel, which was not yet showing any effects from the poison. Then I poured again. I picked up all the empty bottles and started walking back to hide it, when I heard the key clink against the lock. I could have run. I could have hurried to my hiding place. I maybe even could have made it. I didn't.

Erik opened the door, pink from the drink and the cold. I stood for a while, looking at him, then I sat down carefully on the bed.

"What is this?" I let him take a bottle of rat poison out of my hands.

"What were you doing?"

He looked at the tanks, then looked at me, his face painful. Then he made the same motion again. He walked over to the tanks, and stared into them. I watched him. We stayed that way for a couple of minutes, until he noticed the eel start to slow its movement. He made a noise, and kind of fell down, supporting himself with one arm on his desk and staring into the tank. I didn't watch the fish, only him. We stayed that way for a very long time.

We left that night. He was driving west, and I didn't ask where to. He had only told me "Get in the car," and I did. Snot was running out of Erik's nose. I stayed very still in the back seat of his Civic, like when I was a kid and knew my dad was driving drunk. He would have too much to drink when he and my mom and I would go out to dinner. When we got in the car to go home, she would try to get in the driver's side, and he would say "I'll drive, I'll drive." My mom never said anything. We sat stiff and silent and we flinched at every brake and merge.

"Fuck you." He said it quiet.

"This is ridiculous. You couldnt've talked to me? You couldnt've—"

"Where are we going?"

He frowned straight ahead. We drove for a long time, more than an hour maybe, before he answered me.

"Do you know how they make snapping turtle soup out here?"

He wasn't going to kill me. He wasn't going to run the car off some unexpected cliff in this rural grassland. He would just keep showing me things and feeding me things forever, and I was tired of it.

We drove on into the night. I didn't care anymore, but Erik continued.

"They make them into soup. You know how? They cut off the heads. They put the living, headless turtles into vats of cornmeal and they suck through their necks for days and days, just eating and eating without breath or sight—"

"Erik, pull over."

"What?"

"Pull over, please pull over."

"What? Why?"

"Pull the *fuck* over now Erik, I swear to god!" I had never screamed at him before.

Erik pulled the car over to the side of the road and before he had time to take off his seatbelt, I had left the car and was running, and he fumbled and hurried and was running after me. We ran like that through the night, an all-out sprint with me ahead of him by maybe twenty yards.

I climbed over a fence, a wooden one, and he almost caught up to me, but I kept running. I stopped at the top of a hill, looking down into a valley, breath wheezing unhealthily out of me and my heart pumping too fast. Erik was the same way. He reached me, still angry, more upset now than before, and he rested his hands on his knees and tried to breathe.

"What? What is it?"

Then he saw.

The valley was full of cows, sleeping on the grass in the black open. They barely moved, other than an occasional twitch of an ear or tail. The cows were black, too, and we could barely see them in the darkness.

I started walking again. Erik followed, but he no longer wanted to catch me, or stop me. We weren't thinking about each other at all.

We made our way slowly down into the valley, and walked

among the sleeping cows. Up close we could sort of see the gradations of color on their skin, and we could see how big and beautiful they were and how strong their muscles could be in their legs and flanks. Their happiness and contentment lived in every inch of them. We walked on through, not touching them but only watching. And then in the middle, I stopped and turned back to Erik, and with my sleeve cleared the tears and snot off his face, and then he drew close to me and rested his face against my body, and my arms went around him, and I told him that we could stay there, right there, as long as we needed to.

And we did.

DEATH AFTER LIFE

BY ALEX HULSLANDER

She looked around confused, trying to take in her surroundings and remember how she got here. She blended in with an extraordinarily large crowd that seemed just as confused as her. People were looking around slightly panicked, hoping to find something or someone they recognized. The sky had an orange hue to it, as if the sun were setting, but there was no sun. Looking around, she noticed seven large gateways around what seemed to be a huge courtyard. At the top of each was a Roman numeral, from I-VII. In between I and VII was a long, lifted platform where Reapers were positioned, holding their scythes, and floating just above the ground.

Suddenly, the courtyard went silent as a tall, slender man appeared. He wore a nice suit and his hair was slicked back in a fashionable manner. He briefly adjusted his collar and looked around the crowd with a devious look on his face.

"Hello! Welcome to Hell. I am, of course, Lucifer, and these deathly-looking beings all around you are Reapers. They will assist you as needed. Now, I'm sure many of you are wondering why you're down here, perhaps you're a bit shocked even! It is not necessarily a matter of you being a bad person, you just simply didn't meet the standards to go 'upstairs,'" he pointed at the sky, "although, a good amount of you are generally bad people," he smirked. "If you'll look down at your left, inner wrist you'll see a Roman Numeral has been assigned to you. That is the level of Hell you will be living in. Level I are generally good people, Level VII, well, you get the idea. Please check your wrists and make your way to your designated gate. Questions can be directed to the Reapers; however, they generally do not give a shit about your personal issues with your level assignment! Have a lovely time." He bowed graciously and turned away, disappearing from view.

Everyone in the crowd looked down to their wrists and shuffled their way to the appropriate gate while muttering to whomever would listen. However, when she looked down at her wrist, no Roman Numeral appeared. She slapped it lightly a few times before searching for a Reaper. The ones by the gates were preoccupied with assisting confused and angry people, so she walked towards the ones on the platform who didn't seem to be doing anything. One tilted its head slightly as she walked up to it.

"Um, I don't have a number on my wrist so I'm not really sure what to do," she said and held out her wrist for them to examine. She tried not to flinch as it took her wrist in its skeleton hand, but it did feel somewhat odd and cold. The Reaper looked at it quietly for a moment before speaking.

"Hmm, this is not normal," it said in a low raspy voice. Another Reaper came over and looked at her wrist as well. It swiped its fingers over her wrist lightly and an 'I' appeared.

"There we go. You may head to Level I now. What is your name?" it asked.

"I, I don't remember." She rapidly blinked a few times, confused at her lack of personal knowledge.

"Very well then. Off you go," it shooed her away. She looked oddly at it for a moment before deciding that heading to the gate for Level I might be her best bet. One Reaper watched her go as the other spoke.

"Tagi, go report this to the boss. This is too odd of a situation to ignore."

"Yes, of course. I shall go immediately." Tagi bowed their head towards the other Reaper and turned to float towards Lucifer's castle.

* * *

After entering the gate to Level I, she had to walk for about 20 minutes through a beautiful stone forest path until reaching what seemed to be a trolley station. It felt out-of-place in the middle of the trees and brush, and it was completely empty aside from one Reaper hovering by the entrance. Everyone else must have been processed already.

The Reaper gestured to a floating orb the size of a basketball that was a light shade of blue. She looked at it confused and the Reaper pointed to her wrist then to the orb again. It seemed that they didn't speak unless absolutely necessary.

She put her wrist in the orb; it turned yellow and felt warm around her hand. The Reaper watched as it stayed yellow slightly longer than normal before turning green. The trolley dinged and the Reaper moved aside for her to enter the trolley. She stepped on and sat down, noting that no one was in the driver's seat. It dinged twice and began to move through the rest of the forest. A second set of large gates opened up to a city and the trolley continued on for about 15 minutes before coming to a stop at a station. A small piece of paper appeared in her hands with an address and a map.

Hopping off the trolley, she followed the map for a few

minutes and found the home that had been assigned to her. It looked small from the front despite being two stories and was connected to the homes on both sides. There was a small front yard, a front door, a garage door, and a large window above the garage with closed curtains. She studied the home for a moment, trying to remember if it was similar to hers while she was alive, when her neighbor came out from next door and saw her.

"Oh, hello! You must be my new neighbor!" She came over with a huge smile on her face and held her hand out. "My name is Sarah; I live here with my girlfriend Toni. Welcome to the neighborhood! What's your name?"

"I um, couldn't tell ya," she said, slightly concerned. They shook hands as Sarah briefly looked confused before shrugging and moving on with the conversation.

"It happens! Your memory book will help jog that brain of yours. I'm so excited to meet you! My old neighbor was a drag. The dummy moved to Ancient Rome! Can you believe it?" she rolled her eyes.

"I'm sorry, Ancient Rome? Memory book? You're throwing a lot of information at me here," she tried to say calmly, but her nerves were getting the best of her.

"Oh, I'm so sorry! I forgot how stressful this can be. Each time period has its own city and there are combination areas for transitional times, but people are free to live in different time periods if they want. As for the memory book, it's like a scrapbook of your life. A lot of people forget aspects of their life while processing all of this," she gestured to the city around them, "So we get books to help us out. The home is also custom to each person. You have a garage! Most people don't have garages, you must have a vehicle you loved. I'm sorry, I'm rambling. Go in, get settled. If you need anything at all just knock!" Sarah waved and scurried off to her home.

Sighing, the girl with no memories walked up to the garage and placed her hand on it. She inhaled sharply as memories of riding a motorcycle flooded her mind. Then there was a loud crashing noise and it all went dark.

"Fuck," she whispered as she yanked her hand from the garage door and glanced around. "Alright, that happened." Shaking her head, she went to the front door and opened it. It opened up to a staircase that she climbed up to the second floor. Glancing around, she opted to head into what looked like the bedroom. It was full of shelves filled with books and movies, and there was a large king-size bed in the center of the room. Placed on the bed was a black scrapbook that had *Memories* written on the cover in red. She sat on the bed and picked it up.

Unfortunately, every page was blank with the exception of a few photos of the motorcycle flashbacks she experienced while touching the garage door. She tossed it aside and flopped onto the bed.

"Maybe if I touch my other stuff, I'll start to remember my life..."

* * *

Tagi made their way into Lucifer's kingdom trying to figure out how to begin the conversation. Lucifer was generally a nice individual, but he didn't like dealing with minor issues. Tagi wasn't sure if this was a minor or major issue.

Before they made it halfway through the main hall, two children appeared yelling and chasing after each other. They ran a few laps around Tagi before Lucifer ran in and shooed them away.

"Did you adopt children, sir?"

"Absolutely-fucking not. One of the Demons from Earth decided it was bring-your-adopted-mortal-children-to-work-day

136

and they keep touching everything, and I'm five seconds from losing my damn mind. Why do children scream so much? Why is this fun for them?" he groaned and ran his fingers through his hair. Tagi had to stifle a laugh. It was inappropriate for the Reapers to show emotions because they're meant to be composed at all times; they are the keepers of Hell after all.

"Do you have a moment to talk? I have a potentially concerning matter at hand."

"As long as it's not related to children, yes, you can have all of my time. Come, I prefer to speak in the library." He waved and made his way to the library with Tagi close behind. He sat on a red velvet couch and poured himself a glass of wine. "How have you been Tagi? I've not seen you in a while."

"I am well, but I am not here to discuss my personal matters."

"Ah yes, all about your duties. Wine?" Reapers didn't consume anything, Lucifer just felt rude not to offer Tagi any.

"No thank you," they shook their head. "Today, we had a young woman come up to us with no Roman Numeral on her wrist and no memory of who she was. After swiping her wrist, we were able to find her assigned level, but Yelena said I should report this to you," Tagi said. The Reaper watched as Lucifer swirled his wine around in his glass and looked at it like it would give him the answers he wanted. He sighed and took a sip.

"Hmm, that's never happened before. It's concerning, to say the least. Give her the night to settle in and find her memory book. Tomorrow, if she continues to not remember anything, bring her to me along with her book. I'll have her stay here with me for observation while I reach out to the Angels," he fake gagged at the thought of having to speak with the Angels.

"Do you think they will help?"

"If they did this, absolutely not. But we cannot make assumptions just yet, I must meet her before I decide. How did she seem? I can't imagine memory loss is a fun experience."

"While there was slight confusion and a hint of panic on her face, she seemed alright."

"Good. Bring her tomorrow if her memories remain missing."

"Yes, of course. I shall bring her tomorrow first thing. She's about 5'7 with long black hair and blue eyes." They were about to continue describing her, but Lucifer lifted a hand to interrupt.

"Will I not just find this out tomorrow?" he raised an eyebrow.

"It is part of my job to explain details, sir," they bowed their head slightly.

"Mmm, I suppose." He finished his wine and stood. "Now do me a favor and find that blasted Demon that dumped his children on me." Tagi nodded and went to complete their new task, albeit below their level of responsibility.

* * *

Tagi consistently knocked on the front door for about 10 minutes before she answered, looking disheveled like she just rolled out of bed.

"I'm pretty sure you can't reap a soul that's already dead," she smirked at her joke.

"That depends on your definition of Reaping. May I enter?" they asked.

"I guess," she stepped aside and Tagi floated in. They went upstairs and straight into her room. She watched them go as if they belonged here and sighed before following. "I didn't make the bed, you kinda just woke me up."

"It is noon."

"And I was tired."

"Interesting." They examined the room and found the discarded memory book on the ground. Picking it up, Tagi flipped through it only to find a few memories. Most were related to motorcycles, one was about The Office being taken off Netflix, and another was related to a bookstore. "Do you still not remember anything?"

"Aside from that shit, not really. Some things triggered memories when I touched them, but not enough to remember my life. I think I figured out my name, but I'm not 100% sure if it's my name honestly," she shrugged.

"That means they can still be accessed within your mind," they paused for her to speak, but continued when she did not, "And what exactly would that name be?"

"Freyja," she paused and watched them for a moment. "I feel like you have a lot of bottled-up sass that you're waiting to unleash upon me." She crossed her arms and eyed the Reaper.

"I never sass people who wake up before noon." She glared at them before they continued, "Get dressed. Lucifer wants to see you."

"I'm sorry, Lucifer? As in the devil? The King of Hell?" She blinked rapidly and shook her head.

"Yes, but please only call him Lucifer. The name 'devil' was spawned falsely from religions created by man in order to manipulate others," they paused and looked at her clothes. "Change. We must go."

"Well get out and I will, bossy." They floated out and she changed. She made sure to grab the book before heading out with the Reaper.

* * *

The two of them made it halfway to Lucifer's kingdom before she started complaining.

"How long is this walk? I'm getting tired," she groaned.

"Dead souls should not feel tiredness or pain. Only those in the levels IV and up feel pain and suffering."

"Ok well that's great and all but I'm telling you that I'm tired and I'm pretty sure I'm dead."

"Interesting..."

"Is everything I do and say interesting to you or something?"

"Yes, actually. You are a dead soul who can feel things you should not feel and did not have a level assignment. For as long as these systems have been in place, this has never happened. The only creatures with the ability to wipe your mind as they did are Angels and Demons. And Lucifer, of course. You also maintain some semblance of a personality despite not fully knowing who you are."

She shrugged, "You also seem to have a personality despite being a Reaper. All of y'all seem the same."

"We are and we are not. We were once dead souls who found calling in Reaping. Though our personalities are at bay, they still exist." They continued forward until passing through the gates to Lucifer's kingdom. These were different than the others though, they were taller with spiked tops and strange designs covering them.

As they made it up to the steps to the main entrance, the hellhounds stood and growled at the presence of an unknown. Their teeth were large and sharp.

"Dogs." She tilted her head to the side and smiled.

"No." Tagi tried to wave them off but they seemed interested in her. They were as tall and large as wolves, had deep black fur, and red eyes.

"I'm pretty sure they are dogs though." She held her hand out and one sniffed her tentatively.

"When it bites your hand off, I will laugh."

"There's that sass. Look, it's friendly." It licked her hand with its dark tongue and sat happily as she patted its head. "Don't you dare say interesting again, I already can tell this isn't normal. But this is my dog now, thank you very much," she ruffled the hound's fur; it was surprisingly soft and silky. Tagi sighed and opened the doors to the kingdom. She followed in and waved for the hellhound to follow, which it did happily.

"You might as well name it," Tagi commented.

"Hmmmm...Marbles." Tagi stopped and turned around to look at a now smirking Freyja.

"That is a hellhound, a Demonic creature that drags souls to Level VII for 100 days of suffering and guards this kingdom with its life. And you have decided to name it, him," they pointed to the hound, "Marbles?"

"Yes, he reminds me of Mr. Marbles...who I vaguely remember now," she smiled softly.

"I am fully aware of who Mr. Marbles is, hence my extreme judgment of your name choice," Tagi sighed at the memory of the small Chihuahua that was famous on YouTube.

"Have some respect. As you said, this is a hellhound!" she smirked and patted Marbles' head. Tagi sighed and was about to speak when Lucifer entered the main hall.

"Tagi! I was wondering where you were. I thought I asked you to bring her to the library? Why is she petting one of my hounds." He glanced at her confused but held his attention on Tagi. She, however, took this as an opportunity to study him. He was tall, maybe 6 feet, dressed nice like he was going to a meeting, had dark brown trimmed hair, and had an accent she couldn't place.

"Sir, this was as far as I could bring her. She complained

about the walk then started petting the hound because, and I'm quoting here, 'dogs.' Then, she named it Marbles after Mr. Marbles and he is following her. And as far as I am concerned here, my job is done. Good luck." Tagi waved and disappeared with a small poof. Freyja continued to pat Marbles as Lucifer walked up to her extremely curious.

"Pleasure to meet you. I see you've frustrated Tagi, which is impressive given their immense patience. Did you bring your memory book?" he glanced at the book she was holding, eager to see what was going on with her.

"Oh, yeah," she handed it to him. "Not much to look at though," she shrugged. He flipped through it and hummed, raising an eyebrow after a moment.

"No, there really isn't. Come with me, I have some questions to ask," he looked up and shut the book. She nodded and followed him through the castle. He walked with graceful purpose, glancing back every now and then to make sure she hadn't gotten lost. The castle was a really confusing place with decorations from each era of human existence. Though every time she tried to touch something she got scolded.

They went down to what seemed like the basement and eventually came upon a set of double doors with the Roman numeral VII on it.

"Wait, level VII is in your basement?"

"It's the only way to protect the book. I must warn you though, this isn't a nice place to be." With that, he pushed the doors open and her eyes widened at the sight before her. There was a black granite path straight forward and was lined with red, faceless souls that clawed and screamed at each other below, though the screams seemed hollow and silent. Each was trying to make it to the path but would be yanked back by another before they could reach it. Torches lined the room, but the glowing red hue came from the souls.

"This is more like what I expected Hell to be. Can they get to the path?" She looked slightly concerned.

"No, it will burn them if they manage to touch it." He began to walk in the center of the path as he spoke. She followed closely with Marbles right behind snapping every now and then at the souls. "For 100 days they suffer ten times the agony they caused. On the 100th day, their soul disperses and they no longer exist. The screaming and agony is too much for anyone other than my Demons and me to handle. It can, and has, killed Angels, which is why the book is kept here," he spoke coolly, "The book is ahead, it will tell us when you died and give us more answers about who you were."

"So, why is it not bothering me?" She wrapped her arms around herself for comfort. Though the hallowed screaming did not bother her, the thought of one of these things touching her did.

"If I knew, I would tell you," he sighed. At the end of the path was a large, brown book that was placed atop a white, granite pedestal. There was nothing written on the cover and it looked somewhat beat up.

She examined it closely. "So, what is this exactly? The Book of Life, or Death?"

"Something like that. It doesn't have an official name, but I suppose the Book of Death is more fitting. It has the name of every living person and the time of their death. It is the only way to actually change someone's time of death, which is why the Angels want it so badly. They seek control in all aspects," he ran his fingers through his hair.

"So how did you end up with it?"

"I stole it shortly after it was created. God made it with the good intention of balancing out life, but it slipped from Her grasp and I ended up with it. It can also tell a dead soul when they died in cases of memory loss, though that is not common to your extreme. The names of the dead are not within it currently, they are stored within its memory. Place your hand atop the book and it will open to a page with information about who you are." He gestured towards it and stepped back slightly.

"I better be interesting or else this is a waste of time." She placed her hand on the book and looked at it awkwardly before it began to glow. Lucifer gently pulled her hand back and the book opened. Pages flipped rapidly until coming to an abrupt stop. They both glanced at each other before stepping closer to read the page.

"Freyja Dahl, fancy," he smirked, "Apparently you died... three weeks ago? That doesn't make any sense." He continued to read and she crossed her arms.

"In a motorcycle accident? That seems like something I should be able to remember!" She paused as she realized the foggy memory, she had against the garage door yesterday was in fact her death.

"Well, do you?" he asked, slight worry in his voice.

"Remember? I mean, I can hear the screech...the crunching of metal...or maybe my bones? Wait, wait..." she took a deep breath, "I was going home after work, it wasn't even that late, and I had a green light. He wasn't paying attention or was drunk or something and ran the red light and ran me over. Everything after that is dark...where was I for three weeks, exactly? And what happened to that guy?" she huffed.

"For the three weeks I will have to check in with the Angels, much to my dismay. You should have been in purgatory, so it is most likely that they wiped your memory. As for the guy who hit you," he tapped on the name of the man and the pages in the book flipped again. "He is currently in prison and his death isn't for another 39 years," he grimaced.

"That's not fair! He basically murdered me and he gets to live a long life? I was, what did it say, 27? 27!" Rage boiled within her as other memories of her life flooded in. She remembered being happy... "He took everything from me, and he only has 10 years in prison for it?" her voice cracked slightly as she was overcome with emotions.

Lucifer frowned and reached out to her to offer comfort. He never dared ask how people died because it always filled him with sorrow and rage. Then, a thought popped into his head.

"So, change it."

"What?" She stepped away from the book.

"Change it." He tapped on the time of death and arrows appeared above and below, indicating that the day, month, and year can be changed. "You could change it to tomorrow, or even today if you wish."

"That's not...wrong?"

"You tell me. You're the one who said it wasn't fair, so you tell me what is fair. Does this man deserve to die for what he did?" his voice changed slightly; he was angry.

"I think a lot of people deserve to die for what they do to others."

He raised an eyebrow, prompting her to continue.

"I mean, people kill others for their own twisted entertainment or 'greater good.' They have no right to continue living. Rapists, child molesters, animal abusers, terrible people, you know?" She looked at the book and without thinking, changed his time of death to within the week.

"Any others?" Something sparked inside him, a power he dared not meddle with since he found the book.

"You are giving me way too much power here." During her life, she never questioned her thoughts about people who deserved to live and die, but with the power to change it now, there were doubts.

"Every type of person you've listed is in this room currently suffering until they cease to exist. I'm giving you the amount of power you deserve. The Angels won't like it, but I'm not seeking their approval." There was a part of him that always wanted to do what he was offering her, but the fear of going to war with Heaven always held him back.

"The Angels have too many damn rules, screw what they think," she said with spite. Lucifer smirked at her comment; it was something that only people who have firsthand experience with Angels would say, but that was a later concern.

"I agree. Perhaps later we can discuss that more in-depth. As for now," he adjusted his shirt and held his hand out, "I think it might be best for you to stay here until we can figure out what happened to your memories. I have a room made up for you." She nodded and took his hand.

* * *

For the next three weeks Freyja spent her time trying to remember her life and learning the ins and outs of Heaven and Hell with the help of Lucifer. He was a surprisingly kind individual who loved to talk to whomever was willing to listen. He took time every day to teach her about the truth behind everything.

She learned that Heaven was exceedingly picky about whom they let in and that the Demons weren't bad Angels, just ones who didn't meet up to Heaven's standards anymore. She learned that Reapers used to wander around Earth to guide lost souls.

But the one thing she still didn't know was how Lucifer fell.

* * *

Freyja was lying across Lucifer's red velvet couch in the library reading *Lord of the Rings* when a book was plopped onto her stomach.

"You're taking up the entire couch," he said with a smirk.

"There's a chair right there," she pointed to the chair next to the couch.

"It's a lovely chair, you should sit in it."

"I thought we were friends?" she fake pouted.

"I do sit on it, but I like my couch more." He moved her legs aside and sat down. Begrudgingly, she sat up. "You should look at what I gave you, once you finish that book."

"I've read it before, I just wanted to remember." She picked up the book he gave her and frowned at the title. "I don't need to read more about history." She tossed the book onto the floor. "What I want to know is how you fell, because I know in my gut that everyone is wrong about you." She shut her book and set it aside, eager to hear his story.

"For that story, you are going to have to get up," he laughed.

"Bastard," she groaned, but got up and followed him out to the garden. She hadn't spent much time outside, but she knew there was a strange structure not too far from the castle she could see out her bedroom window. It was a circular, tall, brick structure with a large, golden gate to enter. It was too tall to see if there was a roof.

"What's this?" She looked up.

"The Garden of Eden." He pushed open the gates and her jaw dropped. The garden was absolutely stunning. The plants, trees, and grass were luscious, green, and seemed to be glowing. There was a small, white brick path they followed leading to the center of the garden where the apple tree stood. The tree looked tall and strong, with bright red apples hanging from the branches.

"This place is absolutely stunning. I didn't think it was

real." She tried to take it all in and inhaled the fresh, crisp air. Originally, he wasn't going to bring her here until her birthday, which was coming up. Even though it didn't count anymore, he wanted her to be happy and he was starting to develop feelings for her. But, since she asked, he saw nothing wrong with showing her the garden now.

"It is, but the story behind it is not." He sat under the apple tree and leaned against it. She did the same. "Back before humans were created, the garden was the play place for all Angels. They could come drink wine, eat the apples, and have a wonderful time. There were no Demons at the time, no fallen Angels. One day, God decided to try something new. She was always making new creations, so She made humans. Adam and Eve. They were more of a trial run rather than the start of humanity. They were placed in the garden because the Earth wasn't really livable for them. But the Archangels didn't like this and told them they weren't allowed to eat from the tree because the apples were only for Angels. I, alongside a few other Angels, thought this wasn't fair since all Her creations were meant to be equal. I kept bringing it up to the Archangels since I was one of them, but they blew us off for a while until they got fed up and banned us from the garden. Upset and frustrated, I went to speak with Her about it and ask if She knew what they were doing."

An apple fell from the tree and he picked it up.

"But I was too late. Adam and Eve had taken apples from the tree and eaten them. Together by the way, one didn't influence the other. The Archangels kicked them out of the garden and blamed everything on me. They said I tainted Her creations with sin and sent them out to die. Unaware of what really happened and in a rage from the false information, She kicked me out of Heaven and I fell. On the way down I stole the garden and dragged it down with me. Any Angel that stood up for me or questioned the decision fell as well. But I was the only Archangel, so I created Hell for us to live in. As its creator, I was deemed the King of Hell by the newly deemed demons," he sighed. "As humankind evolved, the Archangels set up a system to determine who would live in Heaven and who was not worthy. However, their system is based on who will blindly follow what they say and never question their rule." He looked at her curiously, to see how she was processing this information.

"Wait, I thought God was all-knowing or something? Why are the Archangels running the place?" she asked, confused.

"No single-being can be all-knowing. That would be too much knowledge for one to handle. She was the first Angel, and the most powerful. But as Earth grew, her ability to care for it lessened. She left it up to the Archangels and the lesser Angels to watch over humanity and is unaware that good people are sent down here. The Archangels have a strong hold on what she knows and doesn't, and I cannot enter Heaven or speak to Her without permission. Only Angels can come and go as they please." He looked at the apple as if he were examining it and handed it to her. "It's just an apple by the way, nothing special about them aside from the taste."

"So, why have religions portrayed you as such an evil being? You're one of the nicest people I've met." She bit into the apple and smiled. "Ok, that is a really good apple! Why did you wait to share these with me?"

They both laughed and he grabbed one for himself.

"I had my reasons," he winked and blushed lightly. "You've had so much information dumped on you so suddenly, and with your memories returning over the past few weeks, I didn't want to overwhelm you with more information," he paused, "and the Archangels had a lot to do with what people thought and knew about me. They influenced humans early on about who I was and who they were. All lies of course, but they know how to put on a show. I gave up a long time ago trying to change it. Instead, I try to focus on providing a good second life for the souls who don't deserve suffering," he spoke softly. It had been hard for him dealing with the criticism and judgment of thousands upon thousands of people who knew nothing of the truth. It was nice for him to finally have someone who saw the good in him.

"You do a good job. I'm just sorry people have been so misled. It's really not fair what the Archangels do. Surely, other Angels still question it." She continued to eat her apple.

"They do, and they still fall," he paused, "Poor things are so confused when they get here. Some of the things you say make it seem as if you already knew though. Every now and then you make a comment as if you've had firsthand experience with the Archangels," he raised an eyebrow. He hadn't broached the subject yet, but he was starting to suspect she was something more than a dead soul.

"I mean, there still is a three-week period missing in my memory so that's probably where it stems from," she shrugged.

"Maybe. We'll see. Gabriel is supposed to be coming within the week to discuss it. That, and the fact that we've been changing death times for a lot of people," he smirked.

"You're the one who said I could!" she exclaimed, suddenly thinking she was in trouble.

"And I meant it! Relax, they can't punish you for that. All you've done is given me excuses to start doing things I've been debating for centuries."

"Is that why you've been shamelessly hitting on me for the past week?" She raised an eyebrow and smirked.

"Everything I do is shameless," he winked and stood. "Come, I still want you to read that book." She groaned, but got up and followed him back to the library.

* * *

Lucifer sat lazily on his throne in the main hall while waiting for Gabriel to show up. He didn't really want to deal with the Archangel, but at this point he knew she had been involved with them somehow for her memory to have been wiped. Freyja sat out in the hallway by a door that was cracked open just enough for her to hear. Marbles was resting his large head on her lap and sleeping peacefully as she ran her fingers through his thick fur.

Lucifer sat upright as the doors opened and Gabriel entered. He looked very displeased to be down in Hell, but Lucifer had a coy smile on his face. This was his domain, and he made the rules down here. Gabriel walked about halfway into the room before stopping, his hands behind his back.

"Lucifer," he said with a cold tone.

"Gabriel, you took your time responding to my summons."

"Yes, well, I have better things to do than deal with your issues. I'm only here now because you have been taking liberties with the Book." His voice was cold and stern, with a hint of authority.

"Oh?" Lucifer stood from his throne and walked towards Gabriel, "But I'm not the one doing that, it's the lovely woman whose memory you wiped!" his voice was even, but his eyes held rage.

"Are you accusing me of wiping an innocent woman's memory?"

"I could accuse you of a lot of things, Gabriel. I'm simply stating a fact of what you did. The only question that remains is, why? What threat could a dead soul possibly create for you?" He paused, then continued, "Unless, she wasn't just a soul before that." Lucifer smirked at the slight eye twitch Gabriel made to his comment.

"28 years ago, an Angel fell for asking too many questions. However, it seems she didn't fall here, but instead fell into the body of an unborn child, becoming the soul for that child. We didn't know this until she showed up in Purgatory 6 weeks ago. We held onto her to wipe her memories, then sent her down here. It seems that plan failed though, but it doesn't matter now. There's nothing you can do about it and as far as I can tell, she doesn't remember that she was ever an Angel." Gabriel adjusted his cufflinks and gave a half smile.

In the hallway, Freyja was trying to stay quiet.

"It wasn't just questions..." she whispered to herself. No, it was more than that. She found out about what happened in the Garden. She found out the Archangels were sending innocent souls down to Hell because they weren't compliant.

She found out how to overpower them.

Six Weeks Ago

"You cannot do this Gabriel! Sooner or later the other Angels will find out just as I did. They'll revolt against you! She will find out what you've done!" Freyja struggled against the chair she was chained to. The chains burned against her skin but all she felt was rage.

Gabriel stood in front of her and rolled his eyes at her attempts to escape.

"You failed to start a revolution, others will as well. My only question is how did you manage to fall into the body of an unborn child? We didn't believe that to be possible."

"If you think I'm going to tell you that then you're even stupider than I previously thought," she spat at his feet, "You can send me down to Hell as a Fallen Angel and I will still find a way to take down this organization you set up. She will find out

about everything you've done, and your reign will be over," she said with pure spite. Gabriel chuckled.

"In order for you to do that, you'd have to know who you are." He snapped his fingers and two other Angels walked in holding a small golden orb. Her eyes widened as she realized what was about to happen.

"No!"

* * *

She sat forward and gripped her head, trying to control her breathing as all of these new memories of being an Angel flooded in. Memories of her life in Heaven collided with decisions she made during her life on Earth. She remembered falling into the unborn child's body and having her life as an Angel temporarily erased for her own safety. She remembered waking up in Purgatory chained to a chair and realizing what she did. She remembered who was at her core.

Marbles lifted his head and nudged her slightly, concerned. She tried to lean back against the wall, but something bumped up against it, something coming from her.

Wings. Angel wings. They had sprouted when her memories flooded in, but they were different. She had technically fallen, but not properly. The top half of her wings were black and the color bled into white. She wasn't an Angel or a Demon, she was something else.

Something new.

She got up quickly and shoved the door open that led to the main hall where Gabriel and Lucifer stood. Rage was boiling inside her as she remembered just how much she hated Gabriel for everything he had done.

They both turned to look at her and process the being that now existed. Lucifer chuckled as his theory was proven correct and was happy to see her obvious confidence in herself. Gabriel was now deeply concerned for his safety since he had no idea what she was anymore.

"You piece of shit. You had the audacity to fall me, erase my memory, and now you stand here like a deer in headlights. This," she stretched her wings wide and walked towards him, "Is all because of you" she was now face-to-face with him, "I will lead my revolution as planned, and I will show Heaven, Hell, and Earth what you really are."

"We shall see about that," Gabriel attempted to keep his composure as he turned to go. Lucifer watched him leave before turning towards her and to admire her. He clasped his hands and looked like a kid in a candy store.

"I give up my title, you're in charge now," he said jokingly.

"Don't tempt me," she laughed. "You've done a fine job, the best actually. Besides, I have a revolution to plan," she smirked.

"How can I help?" he asked. He was thrilled that things were on the cusp of change.

"It's time for everyone to know what really happened that day in Eden. No more secrets, no more lies. No more Archangels holding all the power," she looked serious, but there was a softness in her eyes as she spoke, "I will get justice for you, no matter what it takes."

"Justice for both of us," he took her hands in his, "Though I must say, your wings are absolutely stunning. Perhaps something good that came out of this situation."

"Meeting you was the good that came out of this situation," she smiled softly and blushed, "Come, we have work to do."

ANITA'S CURTAINS
स्वर्ग जैसा होना चाहिए
BY MAKANI SPEIER-BRITO

Wow, Chachi was so beautiful.

Saarya, her niece, held the old photograph in her hand of her aunt as a young bride. She gazed at her aunt; a red bindi dotted in the center of her creamy, idolized fair forehead adorned with dark locks and piercing black eyes. If you looked closer into those eyes, you also saw an emptiness. No heavy sadness or elated joy, just an emptiness that seemed to echo in the vast darkness of space in her eyes. No one would be able to pinpoint exactly why this was until almost thirty years later when that young bride would take a step no one thought possible.

You are cordially invited to
the auspicious marriage of
Aadhar Kamran Gupta and Anita Prasad
December 1, 1981
at the Regency Hotel. New Delhi, India

The red invite stated in black cursive.

This marriage was indeed auspicious for Anita, it was the gateway to life of security.

She was born in the town of Agra, a shared hovel with seven of her brothers and sisters. The dirt floors she remembered sweeping from the age of twelve and the power cuts. The dust never seemed to settle. How she sang during those nights when the lights went out and tried to imagine herself as Sridevi, the coquettish Bollywood superstar who onscreen would dance and jangle her jewels in front of her many suitors.

Saarya stroked an old photograph held in a gilded frame. The grainy photograph made out an outline of Anita dressed in a red, traditional sari walking across a beach of nearly naked sunbathers. The photograph was taken right after their marriage. Her eyes were gazing out upon the glaring white beach. Her expression was bare. She seemed pulled out of a different era and plopped into a foreign land. That land was foreign for her. This was one of the rare photographs in her youth right after they moved from India to Holland. She knew no one there except her husband, Aadhar.

Aadhar spent his days driving to the Bell offices before they transformed to the mega tech conglomerate of AT&T. He was driven to make a profit and was eager to one day see ten lakhs (or a million dollars) in his bank account. Growing up, his brothers would always make fun of him and say he would never amount to anything more than a *kele bechne wala* or a peasant who sells bananas on the street. It was this phrase that prodded him to get up everyday, blazing the fire in his belly to grip the corporate ladder and hoist himself up each rung at a time.

So there she was, sweeping the floors every morning at 5am in their Holland flat and preparing his chai for the day. He would be off by 7am and she would dance by herself when the rooms became too quiet for comfort and the emptiness of being in a new country almost sank her to the ground. It was the lightness of her feet that kept her spirit up.

It was never Aadhar.

He was the sun and she was Venus revolving around his magnanimous personality. If he was a color, he was red and she was orange. Orange is considered the most noble color signifying a transcendence to the Divine. She liked to think she was performing God's humble work as she poured the milk over the brass deities in her *pooja* room. The light scent of sandalwood incense cascading in the air. She felt it was especially her duty to balance out her husband's greed, but she would never tell him this aloud. She would simply perform her daily *pooja* and softly knock on her husband's room to say his chai was ready. Everything was kept clean. The sink would be scrubbed, the floors swept, every counter wiped down and even her face polished to perfection. She wished to glow like Lakshmi or Shivani or any one of the goddesses she adored. Her skin was especially a surface she kept to perfection. She longed to be "fair and lovely" like the commercials she saw back in India. Fair and lovely; a porcelain doll on display in her husband's home, but alas! More than a porcelain doll, for she would be the steadfast wife quick to keep an immaculate home warm with the aroma of freshly made *chapatis* and *dokla*.

After a few years of marriage, it was time to continue her husband's legacy by giving him an heir. He considered his children to be heirs, harkening back to the days when the Gupta dynasty ruled over India, he would insert into dinner conversations: *The best leaders were our people! Not those British snakes stealing everything!* Then came Theeran- the brave. He would be the one to deliver his family to greatness once again by bringing them to none other than...America. The land of Coca-

Cola and English SpongeBob! Where everyone drives Mercedes and lives on a manicured lawn in the suburbs with polite neighbors who speak perfect English! He would be his father's dream realized. *Theeran...*

Fifteen years later, Aadhar eagerly took the opportunity to be transferred to the Chicago Bell office and they settled into the suburbs of Naperville. They had finally made it. Anita quickly learned to embrace the new home and its vastness. Echoing white everywhere. She felt like she had been transported from the shadows into an eternal white hallway. She thought quietly to herself *svarg jaisa hona chaahie*: this is what heaven must be like. Naperville was eerily silent, a low hum held in the air only broken by the sounds of running American children jumping off the steps of those yellow school buses. In the Christian schools where she grew up in Agra, she was taught there is a God and that He helps those who help themselves. Mixed in with the Hindi ideology surrounding her, she translated this saying to mean, "He helps those who help their *family.*" Loyalty was upheld above all else. When Theeran was accepted into an American college, the family naturally followed. She looked up the nearest Indian store on Google Maps and assumed her duty of preserving their heritage in this new land.

Being in America was like riding a bike. Even though there were times they felt awkward learning these new ways, they tried to adapt and move forward. The Guptas were so eager to learn about the country they saw on pirated movies (American movies had been hard to come by in India). Adapting first came in the form of Aadhar buying his wife and teenage daughter Ralph Lauren polos. She pressed those polos on the ironing board in her room every Sunday, and the days continued much the same. Wake at dawn, prepare for her pooja, sweep the floors, prepare breakfast, and say her morning prayers.

Then one day Theeran brought home a piece of America in the form of a girl. His first American girlfriend! His father was ecstatic. Theeran met Rebecca in a Music of India class. She was taking notes and would close her eyes, lean her head back during lecture to listen to the *tabla* beat in harmony with the mesmerizing drone of a *sitar*. *Bhajans* or devotional compositions were her favorite.

She excitedly awaited to meet his mother, Anita, to share in her love of devotional music. Anita prepared the entire day for her arrival.

At six o'clock sharp, they arrived.

"Hi, I'm Rebecca."

"Anita," she bowed her head slightly. Her eyes were awakened for the first time in years. Obsidian stones sparked.

They politely shared tea and biscuits over the marble table. The white teacups felt comforting as the steam lifted over their faces.

"How beautiful," Rebecca marveled at the paintings hung up on the walls. "Whose are these by?"

"Yes, they are mine," Anita noted quietly.

"*You* painted these?! Incredible!" Rebecca exclaimed. "Where did you learn? Did you study art at university?"

"They are hobby. Sorry, my English is not so good. I want to ask, would you help? I want to speak perfect English like my teachers at Christian school."

"Oh, I think you sound fine. I can certainly understand you."

Anita laughed freely. It was a laugh that was rarely indulged in.

"So sweet! No, no, please correct me."

"Mom is trying to practice her English. Please correct her. I do it all the time and I'm exhausted," Theeran inserted.

"*Acha beta,* thank you." Anita mirrored her son's sober expression.

Rebecca moved in soon after. Theeran had landed a big tech job and bought a home for the entire family. Anita was exuberant to have another female in the house and even better, a potential daughter-in-law.

Anita began to watch Rebecca like a wild, strange, and fascinating creature. She observed her movements, the way she spoke directly and loudly as if everyone was her friend. She especially watched her interact with her son. The way she was so brazen in telling him when she was upset or when she refused to budge during an argument. It was all so fascinating and frightening.

"I like your accent," Anita exclaimed to her one day when the men were out shopping for groceries.

"My accent," Rebecca chuckled, "what do you mean?"

"Your accent, so American." Anita stated shyly.

"Oh," Rebecca grinned, "I never noticed."

It wasn't just the accent that seemed full of life, it was the way Rebecca listened to Anita when she was finished scrubbing or sweeping. It was the way she fully absorbed herself in every hesitant word that gently fell out of Anita's mouth when she carefully spoke about her experiences. The pleasantries were eventually swapped with an intimate knowledge of Anita's internal life. When their conversation turned into a quiet haven for Anita to express her thoughts and feelings, she became addicted to it.

Anita, for the first time, felt heard.

* * *

"So how did you two meet?" Manav asked from across the table. The Jhaveris were joining them for dinner that night.

Anita had prepared the entire home for the arrival: bringing out the gold cutlery and the thin flutes placed at each table. She even prepared *malai kofta* indulgently rich in its white creamy sauce.

Manav had brought his recently wedded bride, Nikita.

Rebecca and Theeran exchanged a mischievous look.

"The internet, basically. Well, we met on an app," Rebecca coyly looked again at Theeran.

"Interesting, how was that for you?" Manav continued.

"I mean, I think it's more normal these days. In fact, I read that almost a third of relationships begin from meeting on a dating website or app. So, I'd say, I guess we're the new normal." Rebecca smiled broadly.

"Interesting how America is these days. Back in India, it is *normal* to listen to your parents' wishes and receive their blessings. You honor them in this way, and your family. Without doing so, I would have never been able to have Nikita as my wife."

"Well that's great. You look happy together. I don't know much about arranged marriages so I don't have much to add, but if it works, then it works." Rebecca nodded, trying to ease the tension growing in the room.

"Do you plan on getting married?"

"Sorry?" Rebecca was taken aback.

"Is it your wish to marry someday?" Manav asked.

"Oh, gosh, I don't even know what I'm doing tomorrow! But I suppose if the right person came along. I'm very happy with Theeran. I never grew up caring that much about marriage. I mean if it happens, then it happens." Rebecca responded.

"And your parents are okay with this?" Manav asked exasperated.

"I... I think so. My parents just want me to be happy. They never asked me to fill any kind of role or be a certain way. My parents are divorced, so honestly, I wasn't ever planning to get married seeing how their marriage fell apart but...but I'm open to the idea."

Open to the idea.

Anita absorbed those words and engrained them deep into her mind. She lay awake later that night replaying the dinner conversation. It was nothing she had ever heard before, much less from a woman at marrying age. Rebecca was twenty-six, the age Anita was pregnant with Theeran. It was only to be expected Theeran would propose soon. She was living a few feet away from her bedroom door after all. Something about the way Rebecca was at ease with the idea of marriage was compelling to Anita. *Vah javaan hai*, she's young. Anita thought to herself and with that conclusion, turned off the light.

The next morning Anita awoke at the same time as the birds still in the air and the blue dawn light. She put on the long navy skirt and button-up blouse that she had laid out on the night before. After she dressed, she began her day. When she was downstairs, rolling the dough to make fresh *rotis*, she heard footsteps coming down the stairs.

"Good morning!" Rebecca greeted her brightly.

"Oh, hello." Anita calmly replied. "I made *dokla*."

"Thank you! How's your morning going?"

"Oh, fine, fine. Very peaceful."

"Nice. I had a nice time last night."

"Good. Nikita and Manav are good friends," Anita replied.

"The *malai kofta* tasted so good. Thank you for making it."

Anita laughed, "It's his favorite," she pointed above her to gesture to Aadhar's room upstairs. "I'm so glad you enjoyed."

"I mean everything last night...wow." Rebecca motioned

162

with her hands, "incredible how you put it all together. Aadhar seemed super happy."

Anita shifted uncomfortably in her chair. "Yes...he likes perfection," she said, the years heavy on her face and her eyes downcast.

The air felt heavier in that moment and Rebecca could feel the shift. It was a palpable grief and she knew these were rare glimpses of the true Anita— of a woman bound by duty and servitude to her husband. A husband who appeared only to gruffly walk into the kitchen to fix himself a plate of food and return to the blaring sounds of India's "Who Wants to Be a Millionaire?" in his master bedroom. Anita lived in the smallest bedroom in the house converted from an office space where she kept her easel and the fan twirling all day. There was no greeting, no hugs during the day, just a grunt to acknowledge her presence and ask what's for dinner.

It seemed unusual for Rebecca, but *maybe this is just their dynamic, who am I to judge?*

There was a pause in their conversation, then Anita continued with tired eyes, "He...likes things a certain way and if not...he... he is angry."

"That sounds painful," Rebecca responded cautiously.

Another pause.

"Your *dokla* is getting cold," Anita glanced at Rebecca's plate.

"Oh...right...listen, I think you deserve so much love and kindness. You are such a sweet woman and I love being here, being a part of your family. If you ever need to talk, I'm here." Rebecca said gently, gazing in Anita's eyes.

"Also, I think you are an incredible artist. Have you thought about maybe showcasing your paintings?"

Anita chuckled softly, diffusing the sadness in the air, "It is just hobby."

"You have such a talent. Honestly, I think you could have a gallery of your own one day if you wanted."

"So, what's for breakfast?" Theeran appeared suddenly, cutting them in mid-conversation.

Anita continued with her day indoors, like every day.

Rebecca later tried to convince her to take a walk with her. It was Saturday and an afternoon walk seemed lovely with the rich colors of the fall leaves matted on the ground. She was hesitant and refused. Still, every day Rebecca continued to ask her hoping the response would change, but every time she asked, the response was the same, "Too much to do."

* * *

Red paint smoothly glided over the white easel mixing with a cobalt blue. The black line outlined the arms of a red man. The blue filled the face of a woman looking up to him. She appeared to be looking up to him. To any passersby, it may have looked like a portrait of two lovers in embrace, but if you looked closer, it was an illustration of restraint. Anita put down her brush. It was winter and the cold weather allowed her more time to focus on her art. She retreated to her room after washing the dishes and painted meticulously to finish the portrait. For her, there was no rush and her art demonstrated her saintly patience. Every detail in her art shone in the reflection of a pond, the shape of eyes or the curve of a woman's fingers.

The next morning, she arose. It seemed like any other day. She rose to dress, but this day, instead of grabbing the pan or broom to begin her day, she grabbed a duffel bag waiting by her bedroom door.

In the blue light of dawn, a notification popped up on her phone:

Your Uber is 3 minutes away, please be waiting outside.

The home was so silent, her family snoozing in the cold winter morning.

She felt the fabric of the bag's strap beneath her fingers, stepped forward, and began.

ANTHONY'S SIN

BY TOM MARROTTA

Although this story is biomythographical, the names and other identifying characteristics have been changed:

> biomythography – weaving together of myth, history, and biography in epic narrative form, a style of composition that represents all the ways in which we perceive the truth. Biomythography is not our truth simply and mundane, but a writing down of our meanings of identity...with the materials of our lives. We are the culmination of it all; experiences are painted with imagery, perception, and mostly of emotions. Details that become true in the telling.

The chronological sorting of memories is an interesting challenge. My time then is distant and blurry, except when it had been spent with him. Although, we had so many happy days that they sometimes merge into a sweet and indistinct fog. But that may be how I want to remember those days. My thoughts of him may be idealized due, in part, to the intense feelings and emotions we had for one another. It was all going to come together – my future, my past, the whole of my life. I might have had any number of ways to speak about him, but this is the only way I will ever do so.

We were an odd mix, I suppose. Just a neighborhood group of friends that would gather almost daily. Usually within the same several city blocks, occupying one street corner or another. Mature trees everywhere. Entirely residential. Cornhill.

That was our neighborhood and the limits to our roaming. It would all change when, one by one, we began driving. We were throwbacks from Theodore Roosevelt School, K-8. We all lived within several blocks of the school and had attended it for most of our years. Although we had moved on to one of six high schools in the city, three public and three Catholic, we still gathered as a group to share the daily snippets that made up our teenage lives. Carol was shy, so much so, that I found her endearing. She was gentle and kind. A petite little thing with long chestnut hair, brown eyes, and lovely lashes. I would walk her home, glad to be in the company of someone so pleasant and cheerful, before having to make my way to the erratic sanctuary that was my home. I looked forward to spending time anywhere and with anyone before having to journey home. Carol presented a peaceful and calm friendship. It was what I needed before arriving at my home where peace and calm was seldom had.

One early spring day, just after my sixteenth birthday, while walking Carol home, she invited me in to meet her family. I thought it strange as I didn't see the necessity for these introductions. Since going home was my only alternative, I agreed.

Her home was a gray, two-story wood-frame that was typical of the neighborhood where the street was lined with mature oaks, tall maples, and a majestic chestnut here and there. All the branches still bare from the winter. Streetlights and utility poles, all tied together by power lines. The front porch with its tall white columns was the width of the house. We walked up the porch stairs to the unlocked door and as she went in, I followed close behind.

The foyer, dimly lit, presented a heavy oak, pocket door leading into a living room with a single table lamp dressed in a silk rose lampshade with swaying fringe. The rooms were saturated in heavy oak trim. Ivory walls adorned with gloomy black & white framed pictures. It oozed warmth, comfort, and age. A worn, wool carpet lay on the oak hardwood floor and vintage furnishings filled the room. A large crucifix hung on one wall just above a table cluttered with various religious artifacts and palms from the Sunday before. Immediately in front of us was an oak staircase with a carpeted runner.

The smell of cooking with garlic drifted in the air mixed with a faint scent of church frankincense and myrrh. Carol shared that her grandmother lived in the downstairs rooms. She was widowed for most of Carol's life and had always shared the same home as Carol and her family. I followed Carol as we ascended the staircase.

The wall from the first-floor foyer up to the second-floor landing was lined with photographs, framed portraits in long perspective. Carol saw that the pictures had my attention and took the time to identify several of them as we climbed the stairs. The first, prominently displayed, was Pope Paul VI. The few that followed were pictures of her maternal and paternal grandparents. There were three pictures, all in black and white, of angelically posed children dressed in white, one boy and two girls. Pictures of Carol and her siblings' First Holy Communions. I saw three individual ink-black silhouettes of Carol and her siblings completed in first grade. We chuckled, as I recalled my siblings and me also having the same kind of artwork done by our own first grade teachers. Three more pictures were hung of the siblings adorned in their Catholic Confirmation robes.

At the top of the stairs, the landing leading into the sunroom at the front of the house.

We entered the sunroom, and standing there basked in sunlight was Carol's older brother, Anthony. Smiling wide, his bright white teeth shimmering, his eyes had a devilish spark in them as if proud of some unknown accomplishment that only he was aware of.

I melted to my core, my heart beating heavily. He was slender, so young and beautiful, if ever a boy can be that handsome.

Now, with a shy smile, he said hello as Carol went ahead with the proper introductions. He and I stood there gazing at one another, captivated, neither willing to break the spell. After what seemed like moments, Carol ended the trance by announcing that she was going across the way to visit with her friend Janet and would return when her parents arrived home from work. At that, she left the room and descended the stairs. Awkward as it was, we watched Carol through the sunroom's many windows, marching across the road to Janet's home.

Anthony, a shy host at first, offered me a place on the carpeted sunroom floor as there was no furniture in the room. The room was a lemon-yellow, right for a south facing sunroom. It had a closet to one side, a clothes rod running the length of it buoying cold-weather outerwear. In one corner on the floor was a short stack of what appeared to be textbooks and notebook paper. To the right of the closet, hanging on a hook, was a JROTC uniform, neatly pressed, bearing a name plate, honor star, and a Catholic school crest. The room had two outside walls lined with windows and no source of heat that I could see or feel. Brisk as it was, I sat on the carpeted floor; my jacket tossed nearby. He sat across from me, the two of us facing each other as small talk stumbled along.

I was trying to understand what had just taken place, but became distracted by his open flannel shirt, the sunlight gleaning on his smooth chest and small tummy, and his well-worn, snug fitting jeans outlining his slim waist, round bottom, and slender legs. Was I here for a purpose for which I was not yet aware? No matter, as I was beyond delighted to be with him.

I gazed into his eyes as he spoke, probably looking like a fool, lusting after this older boy while he talked, and I listened. I didn't care how it seemed.

I prayed he hadn't a need to tend to some pressing, older boy concerns. I didn't want him sending me on my way. But he proved to be a perfectly willing host. I didn't know it yet, but this boy would become my intimate friend.

Over time, small talk gave way to more heartfelt words, and a level of coziness began to develop between us just short of intimacy. While we were getting to know one another and moving into conversations of genuine honesty, he confessed that he encouraged his sister to bring me to meet him, revealing that he would watch me from time to time walking his sister home, and then watching as I turned to leave.

I now knew the root of that devilish spark in his eyes when I first arrived. But there was something else in his eyes – a gentleness, a knowing – which made me feel somewhat exposed and vulnerable. But I was also flattered, hopeful, and excited. Our hours spent together this day became the first of many days we would idle away, lying on the sunroom floor, learning of each other's secrets, and realizing we weren't alone in this world of ours.

When our small group gathered, Carol would let me know that Anthony was hoping I would be by this day or that, and for my own selfish reasons I would never disappoint. Nothing was going to get in the way of my growing fondness for Anthony.

The days we spent together led to our blossoming relationship. His parents were working during the day. His grandmother downstairs, often cooking and letting us be. Carol always at Janet's until dinner time.

We explored each other in ways I never knew possible – mind, body, and soul – learning each other's darkest secrets, uncertainties, and hopes for the future. The rush of joy and fear, the shame and thrill of our forbidden bond, the secret that twined us together.

The mere thought of him and his beauty, of how he filled me with awe and set my head brimming with hope, made me flush in the thrall of new love. His skin was neither white nor brown, but a sun-kissed golden glow. Smooth and warm and perfect as a boy can be. His dark hair and sweet brown eyes were a family trait. His slender waist and strong legs, his developing chest and shoulders, his arms strong enough to hold me, and hold me they did. Lying next to him, feeling the rise and fall of his every breath, listening to his beating heart, breathing in the scent of his innocence; often wearing nothing more than his small gold cross on a fine gold chain. I wished it could last forever.

There were times that he was devilish and feisty, and other times so tender and fragile. Pure too he was; no meanness in him. No spite or evil. A boy angel. A dream come true. A first love.

* * *

Beyond the sunroom's open windows, the sun was shining, a light breeze barely moving the shades rolled up high on the windows. Anthony was standing barefoot in his uniform, looking perfect as ever. It was a uniform left over from cadets who had passed through his Catholic school years earlier. The blue service uniform with red cording on the trousers, hung on him as if it had been tailored perfectly to his frame. His name plate was pinned just below the school crest. He looked different with it on...more mature, proper, and so handsome.

As he released the brass buckle and removed the belt, he bemoaned attending a school that he felt was less a choice and more an expectation; a life of inhibition and missed chances, perhaps, but also a bearable life.

As he removed his uniform, I now saw the boy for whom I had fallen, the boy who welcomed me, welcomed who I was, and who I was to him. He was not effeminate in any way, but he was far more beautiful without the uniform or the persona it projected. He wasn't timid when declaring how he had always hated that uniform and what it represented, proclaiming that it was a denunciation of who he really was. The uniform, which hung prominently in the sunroom, was always a source of consternation for him.

He would become philosophical, at times, sounding more mature than the boy who lay naked beside me, warm and tender. *Our secrets define us,* he would say, *but we become the face that we show the world. Always a lie, a uniform, which isn't who we truly are. We do it for them. We do it for us just to be able to live in their world. It's not right. It's not fair.*

But, for me, I loved the idea of having something as wonderful as this that I needed not share with anyone. Not that I could.

When I was expected, Anthony would greet me at the door. He would see me coming as he gazed out the sunroom windows. On very few occasions, his grandmother would be standing in the dim light of the threshold of her living room and the foyer. Always in a black cotton dress, sweater on her shoulders, no adornments beyond a black rosary wrapped in her hands and a silver cross around her neck, tangled in the billowing white lace of her collar, and resting in the crook of her bosom. Her gray hair pulled back in a bun. Her eyes, also gray, were piercing. She would glare at me as if I had done something terrible to offend her. She was matronly for sure and gave the impression that she could be a force not to be reckoned with. There was something about her that made me look at her, then look away, then look back at her, troubled at something. Something felt, not seen. Something emanated out of her eyes and was never there when I looked again. I would feel unwelcome, but not so that I would go away. I wondered what caused the disturbance she radiated so subtly. She moved quietly and talked little, if at all, and only to Anthony. She seemed to cast an invisible cloak of protection over him when I would enter as if I were bringing him sin. Anthony ignored her even when she spoke to him. He would rush me up the stairs.

We would relax on the light-colored, soft wool carpet... warm in the summer, cool, yet comfortable in the winter. Shoes were removed on the landing before entering. Our clothes in a jumble nearby, unnecessary until it was time to leave. The sun shone through the many windows adding warmth, yet not enough in the colder months. When the weather was cool, a soft blanket was at hand; a welcomed addition to the warmth of our bodies hidden beneath it.

* * *

A brilliant fall day in October.

An Indian Summer day.

The sun filtered through the many windows of the sunroom. The house was silent, as it often was. We had been talking for hours and I must have fallen asleep during one of the silences. When I woke up, he wasn't there. I knew not to go into the main part of the house. An unspoken understanding. I lay very still for a long time. By now, the sun filtered through the sunroom so faintly that I was worried about the time. Eventually, I slipped on my jeans, shirt, and jacket and made my way downstairs, my feet creaking on the steps. The foyer had a sweet, musty smell. Absent was the frequent aroma of garlic and incense. It was so dim that it confirmed that the house was motionless, empty.

I found him on the shady side of the porch sitting in one of the wicker chairs. He had on a T-shirt and a pair of jeans, and like most of the time, he was barefoot, smiling, but not the smile of his relentlessly cheery demeanor. He had a book, but wasn't reading. I sat a while knowing it would soon be time to leave. The silence was comforting, as it often was when we were together. It represented nothing more than the feeling of security between us. As I was getting up to leave, he asked that I return that evening, unusual as it was. Most of our time together was not beyond the supper hour. I said I would.

The sky was fierce, burning blue, the trees ferocious shades of red and yellow. The first chill of the snow that would fall that night was already in the air. The last summery day of the year was ending. The kind of day I have loved the most. The cold, gray season, sadly, just ahead.

It was dark when I arrived, and at first, I couldn't see anything. The temperature had fallen drastically, and the moon came out from behind a cloud to let the light reflect off the first lonely flakes of snow that came drifting down. Then I saw him, right where I had left him earlier that afternoon. He was looking at the sky, watching the lights from an airliner blink through the tree branches. The night had a chill he appeared to be enjoying. The kind of chill that shivers the body. His fists thrust deep in the pockets of his jeans. A light jacket, sleeves rolled up, pleased that I had returned that evening. It pained me to think that he would have doubted my return.

We spent that evening as we had spent our afternoons...in an empty house, lying together, intimately wrapped into each other, a candle burning in the dark sunroom. Sharing our deepest thoughts, feeling comforted in the sometimes silence. He was his usual sweet and gentle self. Attentive and loving. Somewhat restored from his somber afternoon smile. He appeared much calmer, happier, and more relaxed. He was very talkative when not suffering from contemplating the future.

He sometimes had gloomy spells. I remember well the long terrible days and nights that would follow those occasions. I thought of him anxiously and often, worried that things may not be well with us.

But this evening he was his most wonderful, and I was reassured. The warmth of his nakedness, my security. His tight embrace, the promise that we will remain as one.

I wake up every day with nothing to look forward to but us, he suddenly, softly confessed. *I want to stay in bed.*

With me! I said.

I looked into his face, and saw a change of mood, and it worried me. It was not just *his* future that felt bleak to him, it was also *our* future that felt bleak to him. There seemed little either of us could do about the circumstances imposed upon us. He would darkly muse that he would likely never see the future that he wanted, nor the future that was expected of him. He seemed stuck in a cycle of frustrating hopelessness. It was a twisted notion to think that his life may revolve around the expectations of others with him having little choice in the matter.

He turned to face me, saying, *I just want a life that is more than what is expected of me. Let's not talk. Just take me in your arms. I just want to feel your warmth, your softness. I just want to feel us.*

I took him in my arms and the silence that followed was a bond between us, an intimacy. I felt inspired. He became me. I became him. And together, it was very natural. I could feel his feelings, suffer his sufferings. But also, enjoy his joy.

I'm in heaven with you, I said to him. *Being together is still not close enough for me.*

His response was a bit concerning. *If this is Heaven, why is what we do, how we feel, a sin? You were meant for me. So why the condemnation?*

I kissed his lips to quiet him, to distract him; to bring him to the here and now, away from the conflict in his mind. I would soothe him with caresses, and kisses, and soft whispers. Yes, I was selfish with my needs, but also, I loved him deeply.

He continued, *Heaven is the ultimate end and fulfillment of the deepest human longings, the state of supreme, definitive happiness, according to the Catechism. I wish we could just close our eyes and skip to that ultimate end.*

The clarity of that evening stood out from the rest of the summer and early fall. The room, the words, the embraces, the touches, the moon, the snow, the cold – all of it became a microcosm of our relationship. That evening guided our relationship.

Oneday deep in winter, I came up to the front door leading to the foyer, I heard his grandmother's voice, lecturing him. As I reached for the doorknob, I shamelessly paused to listen...

It is wrong. So very wrong. You must atone. You must tame the shame of the flesh. We are not put on earth to please ourselves or pleasure each other, but to be pleasing to God alone. Promise me...

I knocked, and Anthony opened the door and motioned me into the awkward silence of interrupted dialogue. She looked at me with hollow staring eyes, wire-rimmed with spectacles. As she never once spoke to me directly, her eyes said all that she needed saying. Anthony, as was always the case in my presence when she tried talking to him, did not respond to her at all, but rushed me up the stairs to the sunroom.

As I was an unbeliever in a believing world, I needed to step lightly. Anthony was immersed in the believing world of Catholics – Catholic parents and grandparents, Catholic family, Catholic school, and mostly Catholic friends. He needed to keep the semi-abandonment of his faith as sealed up and hidden from those near him as if his doubts were the end of life as he knew it.

Anthony had his doubts and his questions of uncertainty, but I sensed he wanted to believe. Like many, he was conflicted with the faith that condemned who he was. The conflict extended to include who we were together. He found himself wanting to move in a direction solely driven by his concern for us. And his concern involved a dilemma. His feelings for me were complex and could not all be boiled down to the love he was feeling, but had to include the visions of what we were to become.

He needed to leave his grandmother's presence – that feeling of her being a conduit running up and straight to God's own will. He put on his coat, and we left the house.

The drifts and ripples of winter snow revealed the artwork of the season's wind on the landscape. Within the cold, snow covered earth, spring and summer blossoms were awaiting their rebirth – their own natural future to be what they were. But I knew Anthony – as much as he wanted to – could not tap into that eternal hope for spring.

We are dressed warm for our evening winter walk, an unusual break from our afternoon routine. Covered in winter wear from head to toe, we walked with no place in particular. The wind blew cold from the north as we exhaled clouds of vapor, talking of nothing of importance.

The entrance to the neighborhood cemetery was upon us

and we invited ourselves in. As we strolled among the snow-covered granite memorials, a sense of seclusion seized us. We pressed our cold lips together until they finally felt warm again. We were conditioned to be stealthy in our forbidden relationship, but our secrecy was as exhilarating as it was risky.

That walk through the cemetery would be its own ghost, haunting me with its silence and intimacy – unrelated, yet so entwined.

* * *

As winter shed its gray hold, spring continued to march toward summer. The days were becoming fresh, and clear, and hopeful. It was the beginning of our second year, and I mentioned that as he greeted me on the steps of the porch. He wore a cable knit cardigan, completely open, exposing his smooth bare chest and small tight tummy, and as usual, barefoot at the bottom of his jeans. He smiled his beautiful smile, then suddenly stopped, and I could see his mind reeling back in time.

As we entered the sunroom, he wrapped himself around me, ever so affectionate and loving. His ability to ease my fears, my worries, were always welcomed and today he didn't disappoint. He explained that he only had a little while for me today. My trepidation of sad news to come made its way through his gentleness, his kisses, and caresses.

I must go to a special mass this afternoon. It's a special mass called 'a day of consolation.' I've got to take my grandmother. No one else is available and she's insisting that I take her. I'm not able to get out of it. I'm going in uniform.

It was in the spring of 1976. Pope Paul VI, who his grandmother worshiped, had been accused of a long-time, gay relationship with Italian movie actor, Paolo Carlini. The Pope denied it and the Vatican's response was to have a special mass of prayers on behalf of the Pope called *a day of consolation*.

If it seemed odd that I offered no protest, I can only say that his way of reassuring me that we were still good and still safe, was all that I needed from him at the time. And he assured me in the way he always did – with love, tenderness, and warmth. There was nothing I could do but give myself up to his warmth, nothing to do but abandon myself to his intimacy. It is enough to accept his presence as a gift. Our love was marked with intense feelings of longing and attraction. We had a need to maintain constant physical closeness when we were safe to do so.

Fulfilling his need to be embraced, flesh to flesh, exchanging each other's breaths, my face buried in the nape of his neck as I rested upon him, was all that it took to make him feel that the world would eventually yield to our way. Undeniably, it satisfied my needs too, needs only he was capable of fulfilling.

As our time that day had to come to a premature end, Anthony also shared that his parents, grandmother, and sister were going to Spencerport, near Rochester, for a few days to visit with family. That improved the mood greatly as he invited me to spend those days alone with him.

Our shared reminiscences of our first year, our mounting enthusiasm for his plan to spend a few days alone together, had suddenly made it plain to me that what was happening with us was becoming real, hopeful.

During that time, we spent alone together I may have spoken about the future too enthusiastically, excitedly thinking that we would be spending more time like this and wanting him to look forward to it as well.

He said, *tell me about your family*.

I didn't want to shut down our quiet conversation, but

about family and the topic of faith, which would rear its ugly head from time to time, I had to be honest in my response. None of which should have surprised him.

Let's not talk of my family, I said. *Their opinions and their interest in my life matters so little to me. Their wishes and expectations are of so little importance. Their disapproval and their encouragement of such little consequence. I share nothing of value or importance with them.*

I had been raised as a Catholic as well, but my convictions stopped short of being devout. The only thing that bothered him about us was that I wasn't bothered by it at all. For me, our relationship was as natural as breathing and a blessing. For him, it was happiness or damnation, and his happiness meant damnation. In my bliss, I didn't really grasp that portion of misery that his family and faith were causing him.

What about our future beyond our current escapades, given what is expected of us, he asked?

I smiled at him with the absolute rejection of hopelessness. *I don't see us as an escapade,* I said. And he smiled in return.

He admitted that he hadn't been able to think of a future beyond us. And perhaps his hunger for there being a future *us* nourished this idea. But did that mean if there was no *us* there would be no future at all for him? He was rarely diminished in spirit. But thinking of what may or may not come to be, was disheartening.

Quietly he said, *I'll soon be expected to take the obvious next step in my young adult life.*

I said, *I don't know what that means.*

He sighed, *Neither do I.*

Then he and I and the night were silent.

* * *

Over the next year, I began noticing subtle changes with Anthony. Our time together, most always pure bliss, sometimes seemed troubling for him. He began having misgivings of our relationship, rather its consequences and would torture himself weighing the future, and the possible regrets that he and I may have one day. He seemed to lose more of his cheerfulness as he stressed about what his future, our future, would entail. On some days he would express concern about his family, and how they would feel, should he share with them his world as we knew it. Yet still we had days where he was his tender and loving self. As time went on, our visits became fewer and on many of those occasions he appeared somber, brooding over what was to come. Ever affectionate, even when he was aching inside, his caring and the warmth of his embrace never failed to come through, his tenderness never faltering.

I worried when he would contemplate the nature of our world and our place in it. I was forced to see the pain that he was in. I knew and felt that pain, but I was too young to realize the path that he was on. Though his thinking was often severe, he was always gentle with me, warm and tender.

His feeling that he had been abandoned by everyone, even God, made him the most alone that he could ever be. He seemed to worry about his sense of identity, self-worth, and relationship with God. I didn't see it at the time and didn't know what he may have intended.

When he spoke of these things, there was nothing impatient in his manner, quite the opposite. The silence that followed should have been more worrisome to me. I projected a sense of perfect understanding onto his attitude. I was convinced, what we shared was perfectly understood, but it wasn't.

I was young and innocent but with a bodily ache that drove me. It was times like this that I wanted to touch him, not with an outcome in mind, but with an ache, to make him feel better; an ache which drove me to him and which he felt, too. When I put my arms around him and pressed my body to his, it was to satisfy my ache, but also to ease his pain. Pain that he was sometimes able to let go of while we were together.

Just hold me, he would say.

And I would.

* * *

It was in July. The air was thick and hot with moisture. We should have been celebrating his twenty-second birthday, but that joy had been replaced by the shock that he had taken his own life.

His grandmother, God's conduit to earth, had found him hanging in the closet of their sunroom.

When Carol let me know, a heart-wrenching pain took over my body. At that very moment, to keep from falling to the ground and flailing about in agony, I bolted. A sudden fever was boiling my flesh, the heat so intense causing me to collapse to the ground. Struggling to my feet and stumbling away, not caring what anyone thought of my behavior. My body feeling inflamed, the sensation of pins and needles painfully piercing my flesh.

I ran to his home, screaming in my head, *Anthony no, please no! Please, no God! Don't let it be true.*

Arriving outside his house, my body shut down from the agonizing possibility that he was gone, I sobbed uncontrollably not caring who would see. I stared up at the sunroom through tear-filled eyes, pleading for him to look down at me, like he always did when I was expected. Clamping my teeth down, burying my face in my hands, squeezing my eyes shut, pleading that the news was not true. My legs and arms, painfully vibrating out of control. Electric currents running through my body. Violently sobbing, *it can't be true.* The black manacle of grief closed around my shattered heart and locked into place like a horrible sickness.

Then I knew.

I saw that the shades, yellow with age, were drawn in the sunroom blocking any view into what was, our room. The windows now reflecting the setting sun. I was a spectacle outside a home which had just experienced tragedy. With my head pounding, I willed my body to carry me away. The abandoned railroad tracks, just a city block from where I stood, with overgrown vegetation, providing me a place to retreat unde-tected to suffer with the most excruciating pain I have ever experienced.

Hidden alone among the tall brush, I tried to make God have it not be true. I begged God to take me with him. I promised everything that was holy if only He would put us together again – here in life, or there in death. I wanted to be with him more than wanting life itself. Violent convulsions, my mind screaming in terror and grief, I prayed to God to make me lose consciousness, to die, escape into nothingness where the pain couldn't reach me. I wanted to go be with him. Yelling with such bile, I cursed God for taking him and begged Him to take me, too. I'd make a deal with the devil if God didn't come through for me. A god I did not believe existed.

My cursing at God continued to burst from my throat between calls to Anthony to come back to me. Each wail wrenched the strength from my body. I willed my heart to stop, my lungs to cease, for death to come to me. I had lost complete control.

I was completely drained of the will to go on. Daylight had turned to night, the moon nearly full, glowing in the violet sky, and the first stars glimmered. I must have lost consciousness. I had vomited on myself. My face was marked with tears and mucous and grief; raging that death didn't come to me.

The light in his eyes, his low and soft voice, his tender lips, and the warmth of his embrace gave me hope that I too can be forever happy in this lifetime.

I missed him so much.

The hope I had felt for us turned into guilt.

AUTHOR BIOGRAPHIES

Brianna Ferguson is a writer and educator from the Okanagan Valley in British Columbia. She holds a Master of Fine Arts and a Bachelor of Education from UBC. Her poems and stories have appeared in various publications across North America and the U.K. Her first book, *A Nihilist Walks into a Bar*, was published by Mansfield Press in 2021.

Inbal Gilboa is an Arizona-based, Jewish-immigrant writer. In 2019, Gilboa's short story "The Yearlong Lighthouse" was honored with the 1st Place in Fiction by the Glendon and Kathryn Swarthout Awards in Writing. In 2022, she completed her MFA in Creative Writing through Northern Arizona University, and her work has been published in Punt Volat, JAKE, and Passengers Journal.

Feng Gooi was born and raised in the sunny tropical island of Penang, Malaysia but is currently in snowy Buffalo, New York. Be careful, he is easily startled. You can find his work in Shoreline of Infinity, Hexagon, and Vincent Brothers Review. Connect with him on Twitter: @FengGooi

Alexandria Hulslander has a BA in Creative Writing and English from the University of Arizona, and found her passion for writing at an early age. She is currently the Digital Literacy

Coordinator at the Dallas Public Library working on several projects for the community. She has self-published some of her work on her personal blog, but the story contained in this Running Wild Anthology is her first published work.

Tom Marrotta is the author of "A Cowboy Lost," and other biomythographical pieces of life's painful experiences - intolerance, and injustices, and the resulting tragedies. He has an MA from Union College in upstate NY where he now spends his time renovating properties with the love of his life, and his Great Dane, Jack. His work has been published in the Flumes Literary Journal, Weasel Press, Limit Experience Journal, Coffee People Zine, Miracle Monocle, Plentitudes Journal, Prometheus Dreaming, and Two Sisters Writing and publishing.

Tony Martello is a family therapist who grew up surfing the wild waves of Hawaii and California. He is the author of Flat Spell Tales, Under the Curtain, Climbing Currents, and Of Song & Stitches. His poems and short stories can also be found in The Atherton Review, October Hill Magazine, New English Review, Forbidden Peak Press, Rigorous Mag, Short Edition, and route7 review. He currently lives in San Luis Obispo, CA with his wife and two daughters.

Makani Speier-Brito is a bilingual and biracial poet. Her book *The Woods Hold Us* is a collection of poems about the intricacies of a chosen family. She is a second-year MFA candidate in the Creative Writing program at the University of Texas – El Paso. She received her BA in Literature with a concentration in Creative Writing from the University of California – Santa Cruz. Her work has appeared in several publications including Plural Personal, All the Distance, Z Publishing

'Best Emerging Poets of California,' CIRQUE Journal, Matchbox Magazine, Red Wheelbarrow, Chinquapin and Forever Spoken. She loves the beach, chai, hugs and the feeling after it rains.

Porsha Stennis is a twenty-something year old writer, born and raised in Chicago. She graduated with an MFA in creative writing from Columbia College Chicago where she completed two published works: *Wading*, featured in literary magazine *midnight & indigo* and *The Black American Identity Quiz*, featured in *The Syndrome Magazine*. She hopes to publish her first novel in the near future and to continue to share compelling stories examining the human experience. Her official website is https://thechroniclesofpms.com.

Derek Weinstock was born in the eye of a sharp needle and they've been watching him ever since. He grew up quick and he grew up mean, his fists got hard and his wits got keen. Weinstock currently attends the University of Life, and is seeking his bachelor's degree in The Real Stuff. He enjoys short stories, short walks on the beach, short people (depending on how high-pitched their voices are), and the works of Ernest Hemingway, E.O. Wilson, and Killer Karl Krupp. Weinstock is twenty-four years old, and intends to write until he's twenty two again.

EDITOR'S BIOGRAPHY

Ben White is an acquisitions editor for Running Wild Press who has worked with hundreds of authors, selecting titles for publication, polishing stories and novels, and putting together anthologies. His own work includes many poems published in various journals, *Conley Bottom: A Poemoir*, *The Recon Trilogy +1*, *Always Ready: Poems from a Life in the U. S. Coast Guard*, and *Say Their Names* (under Anonymous).

ABOUT RIZE

RIZE publishes great stories and great writing across genres written by People of Color and other underrepresented groups. Our team consists of:

Lisa Diane Kastner, Founder and Executive Editor
Mona Bethke, Acquisitions Editor
Benjamin White, Acquisition Editor, Running Wild
Peter A. Wright, Acquisition Editor, Running Wild
Rebecca Dimyan, Editor
Abigail Efird, Editor
Laura Huie, Editor
Cody Sisco, Editor
Chih Wang, Editor
Joelle Mitchell, Head of Licensing
Lara Macaione, Director of Marketing
Pulp Art Studios, Cover Design
Standout Books, Interior Design
Polgarus Studios, Interior Design

Learn more about us and our stories at www.runningwild-press.com
Loved these stories and want more? Follow us at
www.runningwildpress.com
www.facebook.com/runningwildpress,
on Twitter @lisadkastner @RunWildBooks
@RwpRIZE

RIZE